# Second Chance Summer

### a Blue Harbor novel

## OLIVIA MILES

Rosewood Press

ISBN: 978-1-7346208-2-5

# Second Chance Summer

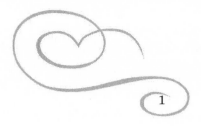

Summer in Blue Harbor was Amelia Conway's favorite time of the year, and not because of all the tourists who made frequent stops to her lakefront café and kept her business going for the quieter months. Summer in her northern Michigan hometown had a way of stirring up memories even sweeter than those from birthdays and holidays, reminding her of long, lazy days spent splashing in the lake, riding bikes with her sisters, and picking cherries at her family's orchard. It meant dinners on the picnic table behind their house with warm pie and melting ice cream, and staying up late, waiting for the fireflies to appear.

It was a time to breathe. And dream. And, once upon a time, fall in love...

Amelia watched a young couple at the corner of the patio reach across the table and take each other's hands. They'd split a dessert—a sign of true intimacy by her books—and soon she imagined they would take a walk along the lake that was glistening in the waning sunlight.

She took their signed bill and bid them goodnight, her gaze drifting to the empty storefront

adjacent to her own business. Not long ago it had been a sweet little stationery store, run by Gladys O'Leary. But Gladys had no takers when she wanted to retire last fall, and rumor had it that sales had been slow for years. Amelia had been eager to see who would move into the space next, knowing it would drive traffic to her café, but so far, it sat dark and empty. And unwelcoming.

Well, no sense in worrying about it tonight. Tonight she didn't need any extra customers pushing through the door. She was barely keeping up with the ones she had.

With a sigh, Amelia finished clearing a table and walked back inside Firefly Café, where a line had already formed in the few minutes since she'd been outside. Her sister Maddie had come around from the counter, looking frazzled.

"I just cleared two tables on the patio," Amelia told her. They were short-staffed tonight, because it was a Thursday and usually weeknights were more of a local crowd. But it was August, and that meant families were coming to town for a week or two, not just a weekend. It also meant that summer would soon be over. Nearly as quickly as it had started.

Amelia went back to the kitchen where she checked the schedule and was relieved to see that tonight's staffing oversight wouldn't repeat itself. Maddie had stepped up her hours, and from tomorrow through Labor Day weekend, they'd have three people on hand around the clock, thanks to her seasonal help. She just had to get through tonight.

And stop that alarm from going off.

She hurried to the oven and flung the door open, almost forgetting to grab an oven mitt before she pulled the now burnt flatbread from the middle rack. She set the pan on the range, cursing under her breath.

"I got those two couples seated and another in the front room—" Maddie waved a hand through the smoky air as she came deeper into the kitchen. "Jeez. Is something on fire?"

"Nearly." Amelia sighed, and then, because she had no other choice, she went to work on another bruschetta-style flatbread—a favorite here at the café, made with three different cheeses from the local dairy farm, and basil and tomatoes picked straight from her own garden.

"Table twelve?" Maddie asked, looking at the order slips. "I'll bring them a house wine to make up for the delay."

House wine meant it came from their family's orchard and winery, located right here in Blue Harbor.

"Thanks, Maddie." Amelia tossed her youngest sister a grin over her shoulder as she rolled out the dough she kept in large batches in the fridge.

Once that was settled, and Maddie announced that the couple was thrilled by the reward of their inconvenience, they worked in silence for a few minutes. Amelia on the savories; Maddie on the sweets. Amelia knew that eventually her younger sister would want to do something on her own, open a bakery, or start a small cookie company. She'd always been good at baking, and pie was her specialty. For now, Maddie seemed happy for the work here and Amelia was happy to give her the space she needed to create and experiment, and share a little of her wisdom, too. Even, she thought, as she lathered some homemade pesto over the flatbread, the mistakes.

Once that was in the oven and the timer was set, she glanced out through the open window that separated the kitchen from the front counter, catching a glance from her older sister, who had just come in by the looks of it.

"Britt's here," she told Maddie. "And Robbie," she added, noticing Britt's ex-boyfriend turned boyfriend again. More than that, he also now helped Britt run Conway Orchard since their father's retirement.

"Is Keira with them?" Maddie perked up. Robbie's seven-year-old daughter was a favorite at the café, and a professional taste-tester, too, even if she was rather easy to please. "I saved the last flower-shaped sugar cookie for her just in case they stopped by."

Amelia grinned at her sister. "Just like Dorothy used to do," she said, referring to the original owner of the café, and its original namesake. Maddie was the youngest of the four Conway sisters, and more than three years below Amelia. "Do you remember how she used to always save you an oatmeal cookie? Claim it was the very last one, even though we all knew she had tucked it away?"

Maddie nodded. "They were the best. Almost as good as—" She inhaled sharply and grabbed the wax paper bag containing the flower cookie from the counter.

Maddie didn't need to finish the thought for Amelia to know what she meant. The cookies that used to be made here at this café were almost as good as their mother's cookies had been, but they couldn't compare. Even she hadn't dared to try, despite all her love for this café and her work in the kitchen. But Maddie...Maddie had carried on the dessert recipes that her mother had taught her over the years from their home kitchen, and Maddie's pies and cookies and cakes were every bit as good as their mother's.

"I'll go make the rounds," Maddie said, before pushing out into the dining room.

Amelia went back to plating orders, her heart a little heavier than it had been a few minutes ago.

She'd only been sixteen when her mother had died, and each of the sisters had taken the loss in their own way. Britt had left town first chance she'd had, and stayed away. Cora had kept their mother's Christmas traditions going even when the rest of them had felt too sad to put up a tree, and Maddie had continued to bake the recipes that their mother had loved to share.

And Amelia...Amelia had taken care of the nest in Britt's absence, tending to the younger girls, going through the motions, trying to keep her head on practical things, and her heart out of everything.

But when this café had gone on the market shortly after she'd graduated from college, she knew that it was meant to be hers and that her father wouldn't mind her leaving her job at the orchard to pursue her dream. It was in these four walls that her mother would bring them after school, to have a snack, to talk about their day. It was in this café that she had gone from talking about boys pinching her during storytime to boys catching her eye. It was a place of comfort and hope, a bright spot even in the darkest nights, much like the fireflies that lit up the sky.

And it was all hers now. Hers and hers alone.

"Yoohoo!"

Amelia had learned by now not to let the sing-song greeting from her father's girlfriend startle her—too much. She looked up to see Candace's face through the window. The woman had let herself back around the counter again, and it would appear that she'd had her hair done today too. The curls were bigger and bouncier than ever.

"Hello, Candace," she said with a distracted smile. It was usual for her family to stop by the café for dinner a few nights a week, but having everyone here at the same time wasn't exactly typical, and Amelia and her sisters were still warming up to the woman their father had been dating since only June.

"Oh, you girls! Always so formal! You know you can call me Candy!"

Amelia met Candy's wide smile, and despite her own reservations, she couldn't help but grin. "You know me. When I'm on the job..."

"Always so professional! I know!" Candy hovered in the window pass, blocking Amelia's view of the tables. Her father was already sitting at the counter, she saw.

"Maddie will be right over to take your orders," she said, hoping this was all that was needed to get Candy out from behind her counter and back to her seat, like a paying customer. Or non-paying customer, really. Amelia never charged her family for their food at the café. It wouldn't feel right.

Still, her father always stuffed a few bills in the tip jar, more than covering their meals.

Candy kept on grinning. "You sure know how to cook. Maybe one of these days I can show you the recipe for my famous cheese biscuits."

Amelia kept her eyes on the cutting board as she sliced through a baguette. As far as she knew, those cheese biscuits were only famous within the walls of her childhood home, where Candy now unofficially resided. Still, she said, "I'll try them sometime soon. I promise."

"I can drop some off one day," Candy offered. "Maybe come in a little early? Have a little girl time in the kitchen?" She laughed out loud. Loudly.

Amelia picked up the plates for the next order—field greens with farm fresh goat cheese and pan-fried Michigan whitefish with a side of her sweet-potato fries—and carried them through the swing door, dodging Candy's open arms and wiggly fingers as she gestured to the plates.

"Can't drop these!" she warned. "Oh! And I think Maddie's already there with Dad." She grinned at her father, and flashed a warning look on her sister, who didn't need further communication. They'd all mastered the art of silent glances growing up, and now that Candy was in their lives, it had come in handy.

Maddie called Candy over to discuss the specials and Amelia breathed a sigh of relief as she sets the plates down at table six before going to the patio to greet Britt.

The couple in the corner was sitting side by side now, admiring the view, sipping wine and whispering sweet nothings.

Amelia resisted a sigh.

"Just a heads-up, but Dad's here. With Candy," Amelia said, lest there be any confusion.

Britt's eyes flashed on hers, and Amelia saw Robbie try his best to hide a smile. And fail miserably.

"It's not funny," Britt warned, but there was amusement in her eyes, too. Since Candy had come into their lives, they'd learned to adjust, to see that she wasn't anything like their quiet, unassuming mother, but that their father was happy just the same. He'd been given a second chance at love, and really, they should support that.

Even if Candy was...well, a hugger.

"Beautiful night," Robbie said, tearing off a bite of Keira's cookie, which sparked a wail of protest from the little girl.

"Busy night," Amelia said. But still, beautiful. The breeze was coming in off the lake and there was still some light left in the sky.

They'd be closing within the next hour, meaning she could take a walk along the waterfront, or sit out on this patio and enjoy a much needed glass of wine. Maybe Britt and Maddie would stick around. Maybe Cora would even join them, though she was more of a homebody than the rest of them.

Chances were, though, she would get a start on prep for tomorrow, and then go home. Her feet were tired, and she was already looking forward to catching up on her favorite shows. And she'd made that batch of blueberry ice cream over the weekend as a test run for the monthly specials...

But while all that sounded nice, the truth of it was that it was rather lonely, and seeing her sister sitting beside her high school sweetheart, with his arm casually hooked on the back of her chair, well, it stung. Amelia was happy for Britt, and happy for Robbie and Keira, and they were all overjoyed that Britt had decided to return to town at the start of summer. But sometimes, especially on these lovely, warm nights, Amelia couldn't help but feel like everyone else had found second chances at love. Except for her.

Britt leaned forward and set a hand on her wrist. Her eyes shone with unspoken words. They needed to talk.

Amelia wondered if Britt was going to say something about Candy again, and much as Amelia saw the good in the woman, she would love to vent about Candy's determination to make herself at home at the café—as well as the big Victorian house they'd all grown up in—but Maddie called out to her from the patio door, interrupting the moment.

"Amelia. Did you need me to check on that flat-bread?"

The flatbread! Amelia muttered her excuses and hurried away, because there was no way that she could burn a table's order twice!

She pushed her way through the tables, back around the counter, ignoring Candy's call of "Yoo-hoo!" and telling herself that it could wait. It would have to wait. The timer was going off. They were short staffed. Usually when the dinner hour was this busy, she stayed in the kitchen, only venturing into the dining room if one of her employees was in the kitchen.

She grabbed an oven mitt and yanked open the door, sighing in relief when she saw she had made it just in time. She plated the flatbread, handed it to Maddie who was coming through the door, and watched her go right back out again, giving her a wink on her way.

Right. She needed a drink. Or better yet—dinner. For as much time as she spent in this kitchen, she was often too busy cooking for everyone else to give herself a decent meal.

She studied the pan of brownies that Maddie had made for tonight's dessert special and, double checking the clock on the wall and estimating that they wouldn't sell out, cut herself a large square.

It was chewy and rich and she knew it would go great with a cold glass of milk. She opened the

fridge, wondering if heavy cream would do instead, when the sound of a pot falling made her jump.

"Maddie? You okay?"

When there wasn't an answer, Amelia closed her eyes. Counted to three. Now, coming around the counter was one thing, but if Candy thought she could barge into this kitchen—

Amelia crammed the rest of the brownie into her mouth, grabbed the milk with one hand and the creamer with the other, and stepped back from the fridge, letting the door swing shut on its own.

And there he was. The unexpected guest in her kitchen. But not an unwanted guest.

Matt Bradford. Looking every bit as good as he did the last time she'd seen him, more than twelve years ago. Still the blue-eyed boy with the tousled dirty blonde hair. Still the boy who had captured her heart at the tender age of fifteen, and then broke it, three years later.

He'd left town with his parents, moved away and moved on. And now he was back.

In her kitchen.

And she had a palm-sized brownie crammed into her mouth, making her cheeks fat as a squirrel harvesting nuts for winter. She tried to chew, but the stickiness made it difficult, and the more she tried, the longer it seemed to take, and even though she was holding two cold bottles of dairy products and had just taken her head out of the fridge, she could feel the heat build inside her, flaring in her face and spreading down her neck.

There was a glimmer of amusement—or maybe confusion—in his eyes as he watched her, grinning.

Finally, she swallowed. It was really too big of a chunk to swallow, and she resisted the urge to cough.

"Matt!" she said, for lack of anything better to say. Really, what do you say to a guy you haven't seen in a dozen years, even if you had thought about him for the better half of that time?

His gaze narrowed ever so slightly and she had the sinking feeling that one of her teeth was blacked out with fudge.

"Sorry to startle you." His grin flashed as he righted the pan on the counter beside him.

She swallowed again, set the milk down and took a steadying breath. "This is...a surprise!" A big one, and one she'd stopped wishing for many years ago.

They stood awkwardly for a moment, as if unsure if they should hug, each leaning in and then leaning back, and oh...the burn! Her cheeks were positively on fire.

Finally, Matt crammed his hands into his pockets, putting that weird little dance to an end. "Hope you don't mind me coming back here into the kitchen like this, but I was chatting with Robbie, and Britt said you were in the kitchen and, well. I wanted to say hello."

He wanted to say hello. *Calm yourself, Amelia.* It wasn't like he wanted to propose marriage. He just wanted to say hello.

"Hello," she said, giving a small smile.

"Hello." His eyes gleamed, and the word hung there between them, the silence far too obvious. She'd assumed she'd never see Matt again. He was a thing of her past. But now he was standing in her kitchen. Saying hello.

She pulled in a breath and blinked quickly. She tried to think of something conversational, when what she wanted to ask was why now? Why hadn't he returned sooner?

"Are you in town for the weekend?"

"A bit longer, actually," he said. "I'm staying with Jackson."

Of course. Matt had always been close with his cousins, and Robbie's older brother was a bachelor with a big house on the edge of town.

She opened her mouth to ask just how much "longer" meant but had the sense to stop herself. Really, it shouldn't matter to her. They didn't mean anything to each other anymore.

Except, by the flutter in her stomach, she wasn't so sure that was exactly true.

"I'm heading over to the pub," he said, referring to the one that Jackson managed in his parents' inn

*20*

over on Main Street. She idly wondered if this was an invitation, or if she was reading into things. "But I couldn't stop by without saying hello."

Hello. Again. They shared a smile. Nope, this wasn't awkward. Not in the slightest.

"I'm glad you did. How have you been?"

He nodded. "Good. Really good. And it looks like you could say the same!"

She nodded, feeling proud of her accomplishments, of this kitchen. But the one thing she'd wanted, more than to have her mother see all of it, was for Matt to have been a part of it all.

A timer went off then, signaling that the last fish dish was ready, and she cursed to herself, knowing that it couldn't wait, not unless she planned to serve blackened fish, and she did not.

She reached for an oven mitt, but Matt backed away. "I can see you're busy. But...maybe we can catch up soon, while I'm in town?"

"I'd like that," she said, even though she wasn't so sure that she should. After all, the man had left town and never called, never written. Just disappeared really.

"So, I'll see you," he said, inching back toward the door.

She nodded, not wanting to say anything more in case her teeth were still coated in chocolate, not able to say anything more because she still couldn't quite believe what was happening. She'd never

been one for spontaneity or thinking quickly on her feet. She liked to plan, strategize, and prepare.

But she never could have prepared for this.

He paused as he pushed at the door, and said, "It was really nice seeing you again, Amelia."

She sucked in a breath, not daring to say anything because this time she really didn't trust herself not to blurt out how freaking fantastic it was to see him. That he looked better than she remembered, and she'd tried so hard not to remember, even leaving his photos behind in her old room at her father's house when she'd moved out years ago. She'd tried to move on, just as he had done.

She smiled and turned off the oven. She watched through the corner of her eye as he went back through the door, and then watched through the window pass as he went back out onto the patio.

Candy caught her stare and gave an exaggerated cheer with her hands, even though she couldn't have known who Matt was or what he had ever meant to her.

Matt Bradford was back in town. Amelia turned from the pass to hide her smile and enjoy the thrill that was building up inside her chest.

Maybe this summer would bring her a second chance before it was over after all.

2

Maddie was waiting for Amelia outside the house they shared the next morning, before the sun had even poked through the clouds in the sky. It was a small shingled house, in the heart of Blue Harbor and walking distance to the café, and the draw of it had been the rental unit on the first floor, along with the big deck off Amelia's kitchen and the stairs that led down to a patch of grass that had become a garden full of herbs and vegetables she used on the seasonal menu.

Maddie moving in hadn't been part of the plan, per se, but it was certainly a perk. Amelia had always felt protective of her baby sister, and being able to give her a place to live (at a discounted rate, not that she'd let Maddie know this) was peace of mind, and one less thing to worry about. So much of her life had been consumed with worry—from the time that their mother was first diagnosed to now, when she was already fretting over the winter months and hoping she wouldn't meet the same fate as the stationery store, even though rationally she knew that she had a core

group of year-round locals who would never let that happen.

Amelia supposed that she didn't need to worry so much about their father now that Candy was in his life. Still, she dropped off healthy food several times a week, even though she knew that Candy loved to cook up "comfort" food for Denny. That woman loved nothing more than a stick of butter.

Well, maybe Dennis Conway, Amelia thought, with a little smile. Really, she was happy for her father. She just wasn't exactly sure of her place anymore.

"So..." Maddie gave her a suggestive look as they began the short walk to the café. "Matt Bradford is back in town."

"So it seems," Amelia sighed, but she couldn't keep her tone casual. She'd replayed the scene in the kitchen all night long, and fought with herself from going over to the pub at the Carriage Inn after she flicked the lights in the café, telling herself that would be too eager.

Besides, she didn't even need to know how long he was in town for. There was no sense in falling for someone who was just passing through town, especially when she had no intentions of ever leaving it.

"Did you manage to talk to him?"

Amelia didn't feel like getting her sister's hopes up too high, which was bound to happen if Maddie knew that Matt had come into the kitchen, and so she just shrugged and said, "A bit. Briefly. We were so busy last night."

"Well, I saw him with Britt and Robbie and I couldn't help wondering if Britt knew about this ahead of time!"

Maddie was echoing her thoughts, and Amelia did remember that Britt wanted to speak to her about something. She could have been warned, if the night had gone differently. Could have avoided stuffing that brownie in her mouth.

Could have spent the entire night watching the door with her heart in her throat.

No, it was better this way. Brownie and all.

"He's cute," Maddie pointed out, giving her a mischievous grin.

Amelia shrugged and fished her keys from her canvas tote bag. "Always was. But he wasn't just cute...he was...nice. Like Robbie."

"Not like Jackson," Maddie said, raising an eyebrow.

"Jackson's nice," Amelia said thoughtfully as she pulled open the door. "He's just...not dating material."

And he was entirely too old for Maddie, not that she'd shown any interest in Blue Harbor's most eligible bachelor, now that Robbie and Britt were back together. Jackson was charming, and

attractive—and he knew it. He'd meet his match eventually, though.

Amelia sometimes wished she felt as certain about her own fate.

"Few men in this town are dating material," Maddie pointed out, sounding disappointed at that fact. She flicked on the kitchen light and immediately pulled some chilled dough from the fridge, wasting no time in getting a start to the day. Mornings were always a busy time, with the regular coffee crowd looking for a quick breakfast before they went about their plans for the day. Today Amelia was making three different types of quiche, and Maddie would work up some cherry scones with the fruit from Conway Orchard, along with the cinnamon rolls that always sold out, much to many people's dismay. Sure, Amelia could ask her to make more, but the demand was important. The urgency drove people here, early, and frequently.

"Well, it's not exactly like Blue Harbor is hopping with single men. Other than tourists." Who, like Matt, were just passing through town, Amelia reminded herself.

She grabbed a carton of fresh eggs from the top shelf, eager to put her hands to work and her mind on something other than Matt Bradford.

"Speaking of tourists," Maddie set down the rolling pin and fished through her bag, finally holding up a folded piece of paper that she'd ripped from a magazine. She handed it over to Amelia, saying, "This is one of the biggest magazines in the Great Lakes. They're taking entries for the top ten cafés in the region, and I think we should enter this year!"

Amelia skimmed the list of rules, which were simple enough, but would of course require some amount of time. A short essay. A signature recipe. And photos. And the deadline was next Friday.

"So? We can slip in at the last minute," Maddie said when Amelia pointed it out. "The winner is announced two weeks from today!"

"It's our busy season," Amelia said, handing the clipping back to Maddie.

"It won't be for much longer," Maddie countered, as if Amelia needed the reminder. "And something like this could put us on the map. Drive in traffic from other areas. You know how cooped up people can be in these parts by January."

"I'll think about it," Amelia finally said, and Maddie smiled as she pinned the article to the corkboard where Amelia kept recipe clippings and ingredient lists.

"And will you also think about getting out tonight with me?" Maddie asked.

Amelia added a splash of heavy cream to the eggs she had cracked and reached for the whisk. "And where were you thinking of going? Every place will be packed on a Friday night in August."

"Exactly why we need to get out!" Maddie tutted as she went back to rolling out the dough for the quiche crusts. "You are thirty years old, Amelia. Do you really want to go home tonight and put on your Granny slippers—"

Amelia laughed out loud at the insult, but she couldn't deny it wasn't true. She loved those big, brown, overstuffed things, even if they weren't exactly pretty.

"And watch reality shows about other people finding love? The man of your dreams is not going to come knocking on your door," Maddie scolded.

"No, but he could come walking into my kitchen," Amelia said, only half joking, because in a way that was exactly what had happened. Her heart sped up when she flashed back to that wonderful memory. Matt. Back in town. Wanting to say hello.

Maddie, who wasn't aware of the details yet, just cocked an eyebrow at that. "As if. I mean it, Amelia. If you want to find someone to share your life with, you have to put yourself out there."

"Oh, and is that what you intend to do, is it?"

Amelia rinsed the vegetables she planned to use for the day and brought the colander over to her cutting board.

"Well, I don't intend to live in your rental unit for the rest of my life," Maddie said.

No, and she probably didn't intend to work here forever either. Maddie had a point, and a good one. Amelia was stuck in a rut. She did go home most nights, shower, put on her sweats or flannels, and curl up on the couch for a night of company with the television. The only thing at her side was the remote, a glass of wine, and leftovers from the café.

She just hadn't seen much reason to get her hopes up and put herself out there much before.

But now Matt Bradford was in town. And even if nothing came of it, she supposed it would be more fun to go out with Maddie, see if they bumped into him, than sit home alone never knowing what might have happened if she'd tried.

*

It had been a long day and Matt was all too happy to settle into a barstool next to his cousin Robbie. The pub at the Carriage House Inn was crawling and Jackson was behind the bar, busy taking orders, pouring drinks, chatting with everyone he knew or didn't know—Jackson had an easy way of doing that. Matt leaned back against his barstool and took in the space. His aunt and uncle had owned this inn for as long as he'd been alive, and little had changed in the twelve years since he'd left town. The floorboards were still dark to match the woodwork. The black Windsor chairs were a contrast to the creamy walls, and even though it

was August, there was a fire burning in the hearth—and no one was complaining.

"Never thought I'd see the day you were working here, Jackson," he remarked, when his cousin handed him a beer. He slid a glance at Robbie. "But then, I'm still trying to adjust to fact that you're a father."

Robbie laughed. "I've been a father for over seven years, Matt. And Jackson practically grew up in this building. It was his calling."

Matt knew it was true. The pub in this particular inn was the heart of the town. The cuisine was comfort food, the lighting was dim and comfortable, and it was a place for locals as much as it was for patrons of the inn.

It was one of the more popular inns in town, thanks to the inviting and cozy atmosphere and well-established menu. It was busy year-round, he knew; safe from the winter slump that put other small businesses out of business over the years— including his father's.

"Chef Tony still working here?" he asked, recalling the perfection of those French fries, and the spicy mayonnaise that always accompanied them.

"Of course!" Jackson said. "Not much changes around here."

Matt went quiet as he sipped his beer. It was true. Not much had changed from what he had seen. The town was just as he'd remembered it being the first eighteen years of his life. Same inns lining Main Street, same small, family-owned grocery store on the corner. Same festivals advertised on posters. Same stunning waterfront view that was the reason that people returned summer after summer.

And why he was here in the first place.

"Where's Britt this fine evening?" Jackson asked his brother.

"She's coming soon," Robbie said. "She was just waiting on her sisters."

Matt sat a little straighter in his chair. When Robbie told him Keira was sleeping over at a friend's house and invited him out for the night, he'd assumed it would just be the guys. Now, he wondered if Amelia might be coming along, and he had to admit, the thought of it was appealing. He'd always carried a soft spot for Amelia in his heart, even when the rest of his feelings for this town weren't quite as fond.

He didn't have to wait long for the answer. Robbie held up a hand and glanced over his shoulder, and Matt turned to see if the Conway sisters still traveled in a pack.

Jackson had been correct. Not much did change around here. Britt and Amelia were side by side, like they'd always been, so tight those two, and just behind them was the youngest sister—Maddie.

Cora wasn't with them, not that he was surprised by this either. She was always the quiet one
back when she was a kid.

Amelia caught his eye and smiled, a little shyly,
perhaps, just as she had that first time he'd crossed
the room at the annual Harvest Fest and asked her
to dance, and only because Jackson was being a
jerk and announced that if Matt didn't ask Amelia
to dance, he would, and Matt couldn't stand for
that. Jackson was a flirt. He wasn't interested in
Amelia, not really. But Matt was.

Maybe, he thought, noticing the way her pretty
mouth curved at the corners when she glanced at
him, he still was.

The women made their over to the counter, and
Robbie rose to greet them, giving Britt a kiss on the
mouth that made Matt officially feel like he was in
high school again. When he'd heard that not only
had Robbie moved back to town, but Britt too, and
that they were not only running her family's orchard together but also a couple again, he could
only stare at Jackson in disbelief, and accuse him of
pulling his leg, because Jackson always did like to
joke around.

But there was no joking to be had. Robbie had
given up a good job in Boston, and Britt had turned
down an opportunity in Chicago, and now they
were making another go of things here, in Blue
Harbor, where others had tried and not succeeded.

Matt pushed back the unease he always felt when he thought about his exit all those years ago, the bitterness that had stung him when he'd left with his parents and younger brother, packed into the family's station wagon, knowing that his cousins got to stay behind, to continue on with their lives, just as planned. That his cousins' parents had made a steady business, that they didn't need to be uprooted and replanted in Minneapolis, where work was steady. He'd been mad at his father for not being able to turn things around at the antique store, and mad at his cousins for not suffering the same fate. He'd been mad all through his final months of high school, finishing it off somewhere that he didn't know anyone and the cliques were already in place. It had been easier for his brother Gage, who was more eager for change and excitement.

And he'd vowed when he went to college that he would never let something like this happen again, not if he could help it. That he'd be successful. That he'd be secure. And that someday he would come back to Blue Harbor, not as the kid whose dad lost the business and had to leave everything behind, but as the man who had made something of himself, and who could hold his head high.

"Let's move to a table," he said to Amelia, motioning to a large corner table that was just opening up.

There was a line of patrons waiting for a table, but the waiter saw Robbie motion to him and gave a nod. A perk of being the son of the owners. Robbie had grown up in the carriage house just behind the inn. This pub was an extension of their home, and for Sunday suppers growing up, it had been the family dining room, where the boys all sat at one end, and Matt's dad and Robbie's father at the other, mostly talking about two things: sports and business. Or fishing, if the season was right. And then there was his mother, and Robbie's mother, who would laugh all night long. They'd been the best of friends, until that had all changed, when they'd left.

His mother had never found another friend like Bonnie, Matt thought with regret. And she'd lost touch with her over the years, too. Claimed it was too hard to stay close long-distance. But Matt knew what she meant. It *was* too hard—but in the way that mattered. The way that cut right through to your heart.

The five of them were seated quickly, with Matt at one end of the table and Maddie and Amelia on either side of him. Wine was ordered (Conway, of course), and delivered, and menus were examined, even though they all had them memorized from years of patronage. Matt used the time to glance over at Amelia. Still pretty as ever, with her long, strawberry blonde hair that was loose around her shoulders tonight, instead of pulled back in a knot like she'd worn it at the café last night.

He was surprised she was able to get a night off, especially on a Friday. The café had been packed when he was there last night, and not for lack of effort, he knew. Back when his parents ran their shop, one of them was always working, especially on weekends, and even when they were home, they were usually fretting over a stack of bills and paperwork spread all over the dining room table.

He supposed it was late and Amelia was already finished for the day. Still, he decided to use the topic to lighten the tension between them.

"Playing hooky?" he leaned over and whispered, and Amelia paused for a moment before releasing a hoot of laughter. "For a second there I thought you'd forgotten."

"How could I ever forget that?" Her blue eyes shone as she looked at him. "It was probably the worst thing I've ever done in my life."

He raised an eyebrow. "Skipping gym class to swim in the lake on a hot June day was the worst thing you've ever done?"

She shrugged. "Should I assume you've gotten into further trouble since you moved away?"

He considered telling her that yes, in fact, he had. That he'd skipped as many classes as he could senior year in Minneapolis, dodged lunch, and dropped off the lacrosse team—even though he'd been team captain here in Blue Harbor. But no good would come from that. She'd see him in a different light; not as the boy she remembered. And besides, that was ancient history. A rough patch in his life he didn't like to think about but never forgot, either. It had driven him, all through college, where he'd studied long into the night and upheld the highest GPA possible. Since he'd graduated, he'd done nothing but work, dated a bit, and mostly focused on making his way up the corporate ladder, eager to impress the big boss, hoping to ensure the job stability that his father had never been able to find.

"I'm afraid to disappoint you, but my life has actually been quite boring since you last saw me. Minneapolis may be a city, but it's not exactly New York."

"You could never disappoint me," Amelia said with a little smile, and something inside him pulled. "Except maybe..." She shook her head. "No. You're all good."

There had been something she'd wanted to say, he knew, but he didn't press. "Maybe you could try telling my boss that," he joked, even though he was an exemplary employee. He'd made sure of that.

Her cheeks flushed and she reached for her wine glass, diverting eye contact. "Besides," she said airily. "Your life can't be all that boring. Most places have a little more going on than Blue Harbor."

That was true, and it was another focus of his mission. The town was hopping with tourists from spring through early fall, but the winter was slow. Slow enough that he'd had to work long and hard to convince the power players at his company that a four-star resort could turn a profit in Blue Harbor. And he still had some convincing to do. But he was almost there. And once he was...the promotion that he'd been working toward for the better part of his twenties was finally going to be his.

And he'd finally leave this town as a success. Not as a failure.

"Blue Harbor is a special place," he said, giving her a long look. Full of special people. People he'd been forced to leave behind.

"You didn't need to stay away so long," Maddie cut in, and from the way the table top suddenly jerked and the yelp that Maddie barely suppressed, Matt could only assume that Amelia had kicked her under the table.

"I didn't," he agreed. He gave Amelia a look of apology, even though he knew it was almost half a lifetime ago. He'd moved away with his family, and they were still just kids, really. They'd said a tear-

ful good-bye. Matt knew that he would probably apply to colleges near his new home now rather than ones near Blue Harbor that he and Amelia had originally applied to, together. There hadn't been an official ending to their relationship, just an understanding that nothing would ever be the same again.

But he could have called. Visited. His aunt and uncle would have gladly welcomed him each summer, and his cousins too. It just wasn't that simple for him.

"Life gets busy," Amelia said matter-of-factly. She gave her sister a look of warning and then turned her attention back to him. "So, Robbie mentioned that you're an architect now. It was what you always wanted to do."

"It was," he mused. Ever since he was a kid, he'd longed to create something and see it brought to life. So far, he had only assisted on projects that did little to inspire him, like office buildings, and a few retail shops, but the opportunity to pitch something personal was a long time coming, and he wasn't sure he'd get another chance anytime soon.

The Harborside Resort was something he had been working on for nearly two years now, waiting for the right time to approach the project development team. The research department had done their due diligence, and as he'd expected, Blue

Harbor showed promise in being the next location for a luxury resort—there was never a shortage of demands for hotel rooms and this concept was different than all the other small inns that lined the town. He had two weeks to compile his report and make his final pitch to the development team before they made a decision on moving forward.

"I suppose you'll have to get back to the office soon then," Amelia said, and if Matt didn't know better, he might say that there was an air disappointment in her tone.

He grinned, imagining the building that he had memorized hugging Lake Huron, revitalizing the small town, and making Blue Harbor everything it could finally be.

"If all goes to plan, I might be staying in town for quite some time, actually," he said.

And from the little smile that Amelia gave him, he suddenly hoped more than ever that this was exactly what would happen.

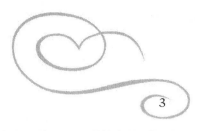

3

Saturday mornings at the café were always the busiest of the week, and not just because Maddie took the day off to bake pies for the orchard's market every Sunday. The tourists seemed to double on Friday afternoons when the weekenders came in, and even the counter service that Amelia offered during the breakfast and lunch hours couldn't keep a line from trailing out the open door.

This morning, things didn't settle down until close to ten thirty, and Amelia untied her apron strings in the hopes of taking advantage of the lull before the lunch rush, knowing that her staff could cover things for a bit. Tomorrow would be her first time assisting at the orchard since the annual Cherry Festival, where she usually offered fresh hot pretzels, or this year, now that Britt had taken over the running of the place from their father, a full spread of sandwiches and sides that had kept the guests well fed and lingering long into the evening.

As part of her initiative to increase profits at the family business, Britt had come up with the idea of hosting wine tasting parties for small groups, and

Amelia was asked to pair each wine course with a small dish. Of course she had been all too happy when she'd agreed, during a rainy week last month when business was slow because tourists had cancelled their plans, and the seasonal folks and locals opted to stay dry inside their homes rather than venture into town.

Now, she looked at her notebook of ideas based on the wines Britt had selected and groaned. There were six people coming to tomorrow's event as part of a bachelorette party, and in addition to providing them with everything from a cheese through dessert course, she'd also gotten roped into a cooking demonstration for a summer pasta that would go with the orchard's latest wine—The Keira—named after Robbie's daughter, and fitting with the tradition that their own father had come up with years back to name all of his blends after his daughters. Her Uncle Steve had done the same with his three girls.

Right. Her cousin Gabby was in charge of the centerpieces for the event, and Amelia decided to stop by the flower shop for a few minutes before getting back to the kitchen. Maybe the brisk walk would drum up more energy. A coffee would probably help, too.

She grabbed her thermos and refilled it to the rim, telling herself that she really needed to cut back once things slowed down in the autumn.

"I won't be long," she told Rachel, as she cut through the dining room, knowing that Rachel would want to take a break soon, too. It was a hot day for August, but the breeze from the lake made it pleasant, and she decided to take the waterfront path rather than cut up to Main Street just yet.

Sailboats bobbed on the water, and farther down near the designated public beach, people were set up on towels and chairs, watching children who splashed in the water. It would be a busy night, she knew, and she'd have an even busier day tomorrow. She was tired just thinking about it, but she wouldn't complain. Running that café was everything she had ever wanted. And she'd be staffed up for the rest of the month, too.

She was just turning up the gravel path that would lead her up to Main Street, and only a few storefronts down from where Gabby's flower shop was located across from Bella's Books, when she heard her name being called. She turned, not recognizing the voice, and grinned when she saw Matt walking toward her, waving.

Her stomach rolled with anticipation and nerves. She'd been happy to see him again, but she also wanted to temper any expectation. Matt had disappointed her once before. She couldn't completely let her guard down.

Still, she held up a hand, allowing herself to be irresponsible for a change. Allowing herself to dare to hope that this time around, things might be different.

She supposed the café could wait for her for a little while longer. Her staff was quite competent both at the counter and in the kitchen—something she'd seen to herself with careful training—and the lunch crowd wouldn't really hit for about an hour.

"Nice day," she said, when he caught up to her.

Nicer by the minute, she thought, meeting his eyes and struggling to look away. He was still handsome, with that boyish grin, and his navy polo brought out the color of deep-set eyes. His shoulders had broadened with age, and he'd filled out all over from the teenage kid that she remembered, not that she was complaining. Her heart beat a slow and steady drum in her chest and she took a steadying breath.

"Are you off today?" he asked, and with regret, she shook her head, wondering what he might have suggested if she had answered differently.

She told herself not to go there. The café was her life, and her top priority. It was her pride. Her dream come true. The one constant in a world that was otherwise so unpredictable.

She roamed her gaze over him again. Very unpredictable.

"Saturdays are pretty busy, as you can imagine." She smoothed down her ponytail, hoping that she didn't look as harried as she felt.

"Business pretty steady?" he asked, and she wondered if she detected a note of more than conversational interest.

"Steady enough." She shrugged. "Of course it slows down in January through April, but we've seen more and more tourists coming through during the holidays. The Winter Carnival has grown into quite an event."

She hesitated, wondering if she should have brought that up, knowing how hard it had been when his parents had lost their business and then—almost worse—their house. The whole town had known about it, and some of the kids at school had been cruel, offering to buy Matt lunch, asking if he was going to be homeless now that the bank was foreclosing on his house.

He'd never opened up to her about how that felt, just clenched his jaw and briskly moved away from the punks who had long since left Blue Harbor, as many classmates had. It was true that Blue Harbor depended on tourists. It was a remote area—not quite as remote as Evening Island off in the water's distance, but enough so that you were bound to hit a few rough years, and you learned to make the most of things when you could.

"Christmas in Blue Harbor is pretty special." Matt grinned, and Amelia relaxed her shoulders, happy to see that she hadn't hit upon a nerve. But then, all that had happened so long ago. He'd moved on by now.

Moved on from her too, most likely.

No call. No postcard. No email. Really, she wasn't so sure why her stomach was fluttering like this. The man had forgotten her along with this town.

"I love the winters here, especially Christmas." The holiday had been her mother's favorite and the house still contained all the memories of those happy days, even if some of them were painful to think back on at times. Still, she had to look back. Had to hold on. It was all she had left of her mother now. Memories. "It's one of the reasons I could probably never leave this place," she said, thinking of the way the snow fell in November and stayed there for the better part of the winter, covering the quaint town in a quiet hush. Most of the inns that stretched Main Street went all out with decorations, and all of the shops, including her own café, participated in the various festivities that the town was known for throughout the Great Lakes region.

"Did you ever consider it?" Matt asked. "Leaving town? Going to a bigger city where there are more opportunities?"

He'd caught her by surprise, and she hesitated, continued along the path around the waterfront rather than up toward town, well past the flower shop now.

The truth was that she had thought of it, after Matt had left and after she'd finished her senior year of high school. But then Britt had already gone to Chicago and her father was still recovering from their mother's death only two years earlier. Maddie was getting older, and she needed a mother figure, and Cora was too young to fill that role, being not much older than Maddie herself.

And so, as much as she'd thought about applying to college in a town near Matt, and picking up where they'd left off, she'd gone to school close by as planned instead, and eventually, put any thoughts of a reunion with him out of her head. Over the years, Jackson would mention something about his life, and she gleaned that he was doing well, settled, and that the chances of him coming back to Blue Harbor were more and more remote.

When Robbie moved back to town last year, she'd learned more. That Matt was an architect. That he'd done everything he'd set out to do. And she'd found it in her heart to be happy for him. Told herself that everything had worked out the way it should—for the both of them.

Only, in her heart of hearts, she knew that there was something missing from her life. The one thing that she'd never been able to find in Blue Harbor again. The one thing that Matt alone could offer. What her sister had found. True love with her first love.

Really, Amelia thought, her only love.

"No," she said, shaking her head. "Not in all seriousness, at least. I imagined going away, of course, but my family is here, and, well, they needed me. And when I took over the café, I knew that I had made the right decision."

"You always loved that place," Matt said with a smile. They'd spent many afternoons studying together over hot chocolates—or at least, pretending to study.

Amelia thought back to those stolen moments, to the simple thrill of reaching across the table to hold his hand, and the way his smile could turn her entire day around.

She swallowed hard, banishing the memory into the place she'd stored it all these years.

"I did. I still do. It's where I'm meant to be," she said firmly, giving him a long look. It would be so easy to be pulled into the past, but everything she'd done all these years had been in an attempt to move forward. Her life was full. The café gave her purpose. "And I should probably get back soon."

Regret pulled at her chest, but she knew that she was just being responsible. She didn't need her seasonal staff getting overwhelmed with a sudden rush and messing up orders that would result in bad internet reviews, or worse—one of them quitting.

"I was on my way to see Gabby to discuss an event we're both a part of tomorrow," she explained, checking her watch and realizing how quickly the lunch hour was approaching. She turned and worked her way up the path toward Main Street. "She owns a flower shop now."

"So I heard. What event?" Matt asked, tipping his head as he followed alongside her. "Are there new festivals in town since I've been gone?"

She laughed and thought about that for a moment, knowing from his tone that he was being facetious. Blue Harbor was known for its festivities, and people looked forward to all of them—the tourists as well as the locals.

"Actually, no. It's all the same, not that I'm complaining. I think it's what brings people back here year after year. The inns have been around for generations, and the restaurants stay current and fresh, but there's little turnover. When someone retires, instead of having to go out of business, someone like me comes along and takes things over where they left off."

Most of the time, she thought, thinking of the empty storefront beside her. The location off the main strip gave a full view of the water but wasn't ideal for most business looking for easy visibility. She knew the few other small shops in the little buildings down her path saw few customers, and only the bike shop had as much traffic as she did.

"Well, I'm looking forward to reacquainting myself with the town," Matt said. "My lens is a little different as an adult."

"True, after all, you can drink now," she pointed out, recalling their evening last night—one of the best she'd had in a while, not that she'd be letting on.

"Which means I can finally sample some of your father's wines," Matt said with a grin.

"Not just my father's anymore," Amelia said. "Now that Britt's running the place and Robbie is the manager, they're trying all sorts of new things." And Robbie's new wine blend was just the start of things. Britt was using her background as a management consultant to breathe new life into the family business, and the trickle-down effect showed promise of helping Firefly Café too. "Britt has me doing a cooking demonstration at the orchard tomorrow, actually," she said. "That's why I'm off to see Gabby. She's in charge of flowers for the tables."

"A cooking demo, huh?" Matt's eyes gleamed. "Sounds fun."

He was looking at her, as if waiting for her to say more, and even though it was a planned party, and even though it was a work event, she couldn't see any reason not to invite him. It was her family's business after all, and if Britt minded, she could always pull Matt in as an assistant.

"It starts at three," she said. They'd carefully planned that for after hours, because the café never offered dinner on Sundays and closed just after the lunch crowd drifted away for the day.

Now, as he looked at her with an unreadable expression, she wondered if she'd misunderstood his interest.

"Good to know," Matt said, and with one last flash of that adorable smile, he stepped back, letting her be on her way, up the path to Main Street.

Amelia practically soared into the flower shop, and her smile wasn't overlooked by Gabby. Her cousin tucked a yellow rose into a colorful bouquet and gave her a knowing look.

"I heard all about it," she said. "Matt Bradford is back in town."

Amelia darted her eyes around the shop, but she knew that even if one of the patrons was eavesdropping, they'd probably already heard the news—and knew the backstory. In a town this small, all the locals knew each other, and Matt and Amelia were local lore, much like Britt and Robbie had been.

Only Britt and Robbie had decided to go their separate ways all those years ago. Whereas she and Matt—

"Matt and I are ancient history," she said firmly, even though it didn't feel that way just a few minutes ago, when he was looking into her eyes, or last night, when they'd chatted and caught up long past the point where Maddie stopped shooting her suggestive looks.

"You sure about that?" Gabby remarked. She picked up another rose and clipped the stem. "Seems to me that you haven't really dated since he moved away."

"I have! I have dated," Amelia insisted. At her cousin's raised eyebrows, she conceded, "Just not much."

Or nearly, not at all. There were drinks with some tourists, of course, and that one summer that she'd gone out a few times with a seasonal hire brought in to help at the yacht club. But nothing serious. Nothing memorable.

For a while, she'd convinced herself that this was a good thing. After all, didn't she have enough memories for one person? Sometimes, it felt that was all she had.

When Gabby continued to raise an eyebrow, Amelia insisted, "You know how it's been. I had to hold down the fort. My father was fine running the business, but when it came to the domestic stuff, someone had to step in."

Dennis Conway had been helpless after his wife had died. He'd tried, but the man couldn't make a grilled cheese sandwich much less deal with all the drama of multiple adolescent daughters. Britt had taken their mother's death just as hard, and when she'd left for college in Chicago, it was Amelia who had stepped in, making sure that her family had a hot meal every night, that her younger sisters could turn to her for support, even if she knew she could never replace their mother. It hadn't been easy, but it had gotten her through the worst time of her life. She needed the purpose every bit as much as they all needed her.

"Cora and Maddie are adults now," Gabby said simply.

"And my father would be living on cold cheese sandwiches and pretzels if I didn't help him," Amelia pointed out. And cider. The man loved his personal blend of hard cider.

"Except that now your father has Candy," Gabby said, and Amelia sighed heavily.

Yes, now Dennis Conway was getting the royal treatment, practically being spoon-fed high-fat, artery-blocking comfort food by the big-haired girlfriend who had stepped in as his caregiver when he had broken his leg and arm a couple months back and had to take time off from work. No one knew then that his leave of absence would be permanent—or that Candy would be too.

Gabby shrugged and went back to her arrangement, which was far too formal for tomorrow's wine tasting, but pretty enough to be a centerpiece at one of the local inns.

"Who are these for?" Amelia asked casually, looking to dodge the topic of Matt for a while, and to get her mind off him too.

Gaby glanced at her and away again. "Candy."

Amelia blinked. "My father's caretaker, Candy?"

Gabby said, "Well, she's not really his caretaker anymore, is she?"

True, it had been weeks now since her father had recovered from the injuries he'd suffered from a fall off a ladder in June that had led to him needing professional assistance in the first place. It had been Amelia's brilliant idea to get him round the clock care—something that none of her sisters would ever let her forget or live down—but she just hadn't realized at the time the kind of care her father would be receiving.

She sucked in a breath and pushed aside that ache in her chest that always filled the spot her mother once held.

"He's happy," she said aloud. She had to remind herself of this every time Candy went for a hug, pulling Amelia close to her soft, ample bosom, which Amelia refused to admit was oddly comforting.

Gabby nodded. "Love has a way of making people happy. Look at you, for example. You're practically glowing. In fact, I don't think I've ever seen your cheeks quite so rosy or your eyes quite so shiny." She gave a pert smile.

"Very funny," Amelia remarked.

"Why deny it?" Gabby slid the bouquet to the side. Amelia didn't even want to think about what the card read. Candy was very fond of pet names, and her father had obliged. "You and Matt were pretty crazy about each other back in high school."

Amelia nodded. "We were. But that was over twelve years ago."

"So?"

Amelia stared at her cousin, who could be almost more infuriating than her sisters at times, mostly because unlike her sisters, she saw Gabby as a peer, whereas her sisters saw her as someone who had taken their mother's place in many ways, starting with the daily cooking. The way Amelia saw it, she couldn't offer her family much else, but a hot meal after a long, rough day was good for the soul, and it helped her to feel better too.

It was something she could control, and the act of slicing vegetables, following the steps of a recipe, and seeing the smile that so rarely graced her father's face otherwise, was her own sort of therapy.

"So..." She blinked rapidly, struggling to land on the best excuse. "So he never called or reached out. And he doesn't even live here. He has a career and an entire life in another city."

Gabby just tutted. "You are entirely too practical for your own good, Amelia Conway. Next thing I know you'll be telling me that sending someone flowers is a pointless exercise, too."

"Well, they don't exactly last very long," Amelia pointed out, only half-joking.

Gabby wagged a finger at her. "What you need, dear cousin of mine, is someone to come into town and sweep you off your feet and show you that love is magical and lasting and that it doesn't always fit neatly into our lives."

Amelia leaned a hip against the counter. "And you're speaking from experience, are you?"

At this, Gabby faltered. She jutted her chin, and resumed clipping rose stems. "I am speaking from experience, yes. Just not the firsthand kind."

Amelia laughed. Gabby had always loved watching romantic comedies and reading romance novels on lazy summer afternoons. She was one of the prettiest girls in school, who could have had her pick of any of the local guys, but she claimed none of them really did it for her.

Amelia wasn't so sure about that. She'd seen the way Gabby looked at Jackson Bradford, who was too busy flirting with anyone who passed through town to settle down.

But Gabby had never let on, and so Amelia said nothing. Unlike her cousin, she didn't see a reason to pry into other people's love lives, but it would be nice to have one of her own, wouldn't it? And Matt did say that if his plans worked out that he

might be staying in Blue Harbor for quite some time.

The question was, just what were those plans exactly?

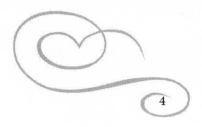

4

Britt was already stationed near the big red barn that was the hallmark of Conway Orchard when Amelia pulled up at two o'clock—leaving plenty of time to set up for the wine tasting and the cooking demonstration. Granted, she'd had to all but shoo a few strays from the café so she could close up for the day. Old Lenny could sit at his usual table for hours with the Sunday paper. But when she'd offered him a free cup of coffee first thing Tuesday when the café reopened, he was quick to go.

"Gabby dropped off the flowers at the market this morning," Britt told her as they took trips unloading the trays of food and pans and plastic containers of prepped ingredients that Amelia would be using. She'd carefully measured everything in advance, knowing that there wasn't a kitchen she could run to if she forgot anything. "And Maddie went over to visit Dad. I couldn't exactly say no."

"It's fine," Amelia said briskly. "I didn't ask her to help out and I'm sure Dad will be happy to see her. Did she save him a pie?"

Britt grinned. "Of course."

Their youngest sister was still selling a dozen or so freshly made pies with the fruits directly from this orchard at the Sunday morning market, just like their mother had done every Sunday of their childhoods, and, like Maddie, always saving one for their Sunday family dinner.

Sundays were one of the happiest days in their week growing up. No matter the season or the weather, the entire family headed straight to the market in the old converted barn to begin setting up the sales for the day, mostly pints of fruits grown on the land, and jams and ciders, too. Over the years, it had grown, and now Gabby sold some lovely floral arrangements. Tourists stopped in, sure, but the market was a local hotspot. This was where people came week after week.

It was tradition. And folks in Blue Harbor valued tradition. She certainly did.

Britt lowered her voice to a whisper as they walked deeper into the rows of grape bushes at the back of the property: the vineyard that her father and uncle had planted with their own two hands. "As a heads-up, the bachelorette party is already here—and they may already be a little inebriated."

"May?" Amelia grinned. She didn't have much personal experience with bachelorette parties—none of her sisters were married and only one of her cousins had tied the knot (and promptly untied it). Few of her friends from school had stayed in town after graduation, and those that remained had either married young or were still waiting for their happy ending.

"So I assume that I should probably get the cheese plate ready before we start the pairings," she said as they set the last of the trays on the prep station that faced a lovely picnic table set up with bright local flowers and candles and a breathtaking view of the vineyard with the barn off in the distance—possibly the best spot on the land. "Anything else you should warn me about?"

"Only that Candy was already asking about the guy she saw at the café the other night."

Of course. It was probably Candy's mission this morning at the market.

"What did you tell her?" she asked, even though she knew that Britt would have her back.

Britt patted her on the shoulder. "Just that he was Robbie's cousin."

Sadly, that probably only made Candy more curious.

"Well, there's nothing to tell," Amelia said.

Britt raised an eyebrow. "If you say so."

Amelia shook her head and began assembling the cheese, crackers, and bread on a round wooden tray, and reached for the baskets of freshly picked berries and grapes that Britt had already brought over before she'd arrived. The brie had warmed naturally in the summer sun, and she added a drizzle of homemade caramel and crushed pecans that went well with the plump blackberries. Her stomach grumbled and she resisted the urge to taste test. Maybe back in her own kitchen she would, but not here. Not with Britt pacing back and forth like she was doing now, checking her phone every few seconds. Really, when it came to worrying, the oldest of the sisters won the prize.

She caught her sister's eye, not liking the way Britt seemed to suddenly be fighting off some secret smile as she set both hands on the work table and locked her gaze. Amelia set down the baguette she had started to slice, her heart skipping a beat.

"Please tell me Candy isn't here!" she said, and to her relief, Britt shook her head, laughing. "Don't you think I would have all but shouted that?"

It was true, when it came to Candy, they were a united force. They saw the good in the woman, but they were still adjusting. And Candy wasn't exactly one for easing into things.

"But there is a visitor," Britt continued. She waggled her eyebrows suggestively. "Matt's here. Robbie just texted me."

Amelia tried to feign nonchalance but she couldn't deny the pleasure she felt. So he had come! When she'd casually mentioned the event, she couldn't be sure that he'd actually taken the invitation seriously.

Then again, his cousin was the manager of the place. And it was market day. And...

Her mouth felt dry. It *was* possible that he'd come to see her.

Nervously, she went about setting up the rest of the plates as Britt counted out glasses and set up the wine bottles in the order that she would open them. Amelia's eyes kept drifting toward the various barn-style buildings at the edge of the rows of grapes, looking for a glance of Matt under the pretense of keeping an eye out for the group of women who should really be her top priority at the moment. Really! This was a chance to shine! To show off what she did best. To try her skills at something new and exciting. Something that could be a win for both her and Britt if it went off well.

Britt was clearly anxious—as evidenced by the return of the tight bun that she had worn in her corporate days and then abandoned after returning to the low-key lifestyle that made Blue Harbor so appealing. Today Amelia noted that her sister's nails were freshly manicured, not a strand of hair was out of place, and she was wearing heeled espadrilles with a white linen shift dress.

Amelia, on the other hand, hadn't exactly considered her appearance when she'd planned for the day. At least, not too much. Sure, the thought of Matt bloomed, as it had every day since he'd walked into her kitchen, but she needed to be

functional, not just presentable. Like her sister, she'd pulled her hair back, as she always did when she was working with food, but the similarities stopped there. Her legs were covered in grass green capris. She wore her favorite canvas sneakers that were comfortable for a long day on her feet. And she fully intended to cover her simple white tee with an apron.

Britt seemed too busy fussing over the details of the tablescape and cross-checking her lists to concern herself with Amelia—or the fact that a group of giggling women was now headed their way. Or rather, teetering.

Amelia pulled herself up straight and put Matt right out of her mind. The guests had arrived, and customers always came first. She was here to plate her dishes and present a little cooking demo using the orchard's wine and fresh fruit. She was not here to dart her eyes all over the property in the hopes of seeing Matt again.

Still, as the women settled into their table and tasted their first wine, which Britt had clearly spent a lot of time tasting so that she could describe it in such vivid detail that Amelia could practically taste it without sampling any, and Amelia passed around the food pairings, she couldn't help but catch the ring on the bride to be's finger and feel an internal twitch at the sight of it.

Her own hands were bare, free of any polish because she would just nick a manicure in the kitchen, and, well, neglected looking. She made a point to give them a little pampering when she went home tonight, and not because Matt Bradford was in town. Gabby was right when she said that Amelia was often too practical for her own good. She might use her hands for nearly every minute of her waking hours prepping food, but that didn't mean she couldn't enjoy a little polish now and then.

She'd book a manicure tomorrow on her day off, she decided. A treat for all her hard work today.

The first pairing went off smoothly, even though some of the women only picked at their food and asked for refills of the wine. Amelia knew better than to take it personally—she knew that she'd never be able to maintain those slim figures if she tasted all of the rich foods she made, and despite always keeping a focus on healthy and fresh, she wasn't one to skimp on flavors that enhanced a dish. She supposed that was why she had shapely hips and hadn't been seen wearing a two-piece bathing suit since the age of twelve.

Not that Matt had ever complained.

She darted her eyes back to the main building of the business, even though she couldn't be sure that Matt was in there or if he'd left. He'd come early.

He'd probably come to see Robbie. She scolded herself as she prepped the last of the plates, so that she could get started on everything she would need for the demo.

And that was when he must have snuck up on her, tapping her on the shoulder, right as she was reaching for the serrated knife to cut through the remainder of the crusty baguette she saved to use for the dessert bruschetta recipe featuring summer cherries soaked in one of their best-selling red wines.

The knife came dangerously close to cutting the hand she had just intended to make so pretty the next day, and she was quick enough to release it, sending it flying down into the grass.

She gave him a pointed look. "Good thing that wasn't a steak knife or I can't be sure I'd still have all five toes."

He laughed. God, he had the best laugh. Deep and smooth and so familiar.

"I didn't mean to startle you. Just thought I'd see how it was going."

The women at the table had quieted down now, as they all took in the two men who had come to join them. Amelia couldn't blame them—after all, they couldn't all be engaged like the guest of honor, and the Bradford men were something of a legend here in Blue Harbor. One of the particularly pretty women stood and sauntered over to where

Amelia had prepped her ingredients for the demo, her eyes never straying from Matt as she reached down and plucked a cherry from Amelia's bowl and popped it into her mouth.

"Hi," she said, a little breathlessly, her eyes only on Matt.

Amelia could feel the heat of anger and humiliation in her face. These girls were all dressed up, with long hair and perfume wafting over the cooking smells, and gold necklaces and cute little summer outfits. And Matt was a man. A very unattached man.

At least—she assumed he was. She realized that was one detail she hadn't directly asked, not that he had mentioned anything about a girlfriend back in Minneapolis. Robbie never had either, unless he had intentionally omitted that information.

She held her breath, waiting to see how Matt would respond, but after a beat he simply said, "Enjoy the party," with a polite smile, and before she could even fully feel the swell of relief when she saw the disappointment shadow the other girl's face, he set a hand on her wrist and said, "Do you have an extra apron?"

Her wrist warmed under his touch, and it was only then that she realized just how long it had been since she had been touched. Or held. By someone other than Candy, that was.

She always carried a spare apron in case of accidents, and she could barely suppress her smile as she pulled one from the canvas tote she carried with her to and from work. And, really, everywhere else.

Practical. Just like Gabby had said.

The other women at the party all had cute little handbags, she noticed. Some had gold chains for straps. Some were even fun colors. Like pink. She had the strange desire to own a pink handbag, even if it did seem frivolous, or worse—like something Candy might carry. Usually, she poured all her income back into the café.

"Looks like we'd better get these ladies some food before they eat me alive," Matt said with a flash of a grin.

"You might be spared. Looks like they've moved on to Robbie now," Amelia said with a laugh as she handed him the bowl of cherries, still irked that her carefully measured ingredients had been cut short.

Sure enough, the women were all fawning over Robbie, peppering him with questions about his role here on the orchard and admiring the tan that came with working out of doors so much during peak season. Amelia could practically count down the seconds until one of them commented on the size of his biceps. If only they knew he spent the majority of his time behind a computer screen and the rest at home with his young daughter.

Britt didn't try to stop them, but merely caught Amelia's eye and moved hers skyward, before briskly walking over to the demo stand, which was nothing more than an old farmer's bench complete with two burners.

Amelia added a drizzle of olive oil to one of the pans and waited for it to heat. Matt was standing beside her, looking rather adorable in the blue striped apron that everyone at the café wore. "After you slice the bread, you can grill it in this pan."

She handed him the one she'd set aside for the toast and glanced at Britt, who was watching her in obvious amusement.

"You seem more relaxed," Amelia remarked. She began pitting cherries—something she could probably do with her eyes closed after all the years of her childhood spent taking on the task.

Britt shrugged. "Those women don't bother me. They're just having fun, and that's what we want, right? If you ask me, this is turning out to be a major success. I'm thinking we should book as many as we can, provided you're up for it? We might get a few groups at once, or a second set in the early evening?"

Always thinking two steps ahead, that sister of hers.

"So long as I can make it work around my schedule at the café, I'm not in a position to say no," Amelia said. She saw Matt frowning at her and, assuming he needed further instruction, handed over the cherries she'd already pitted. "Chopped, not diced, please."

His eyes glimmered. "Is there a difference? Kidding," he said, when he got the reaction he was looking for. "I'm actually pretty good in the kitchen. Years of being a bachelor will turn any man into a chef."

Amelia slid her gaze back to Britt, who clearly hadn't missed that statement any more than Amelia had. She muttered an excuse about the guests and went back to the table, where Robbie was clearly looking flustered by all the attention.

Amelia uncorked a bottle of the wine she was using in the cherry reduction and set it aside to breathe.

"So, a bachelor? I guess that's why you don't need to run off any time soon."

"Just one of the reasons," he said, giving her a look that made her stomach flip over.

He finished chopping the cherries as she passed them to him, doing an even and fine cut, if she did say so herself. But then, they'd always worked well together. Always had an easy relationship that had been one of the highlights of an otherwise rough time in her past, when her mother was sick and then passed, when she felt like the weight of her entire household was on her shoulders. With Matt, she could still be Amelia. Amelia who didn't have two younger sisters relying on her to fill the space that their mother once held. Amelia who didn't know how to make her father happy or how to even help him other than to stay busy in the kitchen.

"You know," she said as she prepped the last few ingredients. The demo would begin soon, and judging from the hooting and hollering now going on with the bachelorette party, she couldn't get to it soon enough. "I could always give you a job at the café if you decide to stick around."

He laughed. "That's a tempting offer. But I meant what I said the other night. If things go according to plan, I could be spending a lot more time here, overseeing a new project."

"A new project in Blue Harbor?" Well, this was certainly interesting.

He gave her a little smile. "That's the plan. But it hasn't been approved yet."

She nodded. He probably couldn't share too much then. "Do you think it will be approved?"

She was holding her breath, she realized, wanting this for him probably as much as he wanted it for himself. Having him here, standing beside her, so close that she could feel the heat from his skin

and imagine what it might be like to touch him again felt too good to lose again.

"If I have anything to do with it, I won't be going back to Minneapolis for my final pitch without being absolutely certain the project will be approved."

"My! You sound determined!"

When he met her eyes, his gaze was intense. "I am determined. This is my second chance with this town. And I intend to make the most of it."

So did she, Amelia thought.

*

The women from the party were long gone, leaving a table of empty wine glasses, a few plates of uneaten food (though not many, because it seemed all the libations had eventually weakened whatever resolves they harbored for dietary restrictions) and smiles on the faces of everyone who had a part in making this event a success.

"I think this calls for a toast!" Britt said, reaching for one of the unopened bottles of wine. Robbie quickly gathered up four glasses, and Amelia glanced at Matt who nodded eagerly.

"Why not?" Amelia said, getting caught up in the moment. She had the evening off, and tomorrow too. So what if she usually used this time to meal prep and menu plan and grocery shop? She usually did her laundry on Sunday evenings, too, not that she'd be sharing that bit tonight. Matt may be a bachelor, but that didn't mean he didn't have a social life. Or date.

And really, the mere thought of him dating shouldn't make her stomach go all funny like that. He was a thirty-year-old man. She'd been his high school sweetheart. Chances were that he'd found a college sweetheart, too. That she was just a part of his past, much like this town.

"I suppose that my clean-up can wait," she said, taking a glass. It was cool and sharp, and she didn't even realize how hot she had become standing over those burners in the late afternoon sun until she took a sip.

It went straight to her head, and she was all too happy when Matt motioned to the Adirondack chairs set up near the back of one of the barns.

"So, do you think you'll do this again?" Matt asked Britt and Amelia as they walked single file through the vineyard.

It was Robbie who answered, saying, "I don't see why not."

Britt gave him a rueful grin over her shoulder. "You're just saying that because you had six women flirting with you."

"Five." Robbie grinned. "One of them was engaged, remember?"

Britt just shook her head. She was secure in the relationship by now. They'd committed to each other, even if the words weren't yet official. But Britt hadn't taken their reunion lightly, and neither had Robbie. And now, they weren't just back together in the romantic sense, but they were also all but running the orchard together, even if technically their father had left it to Britt.

"Well, they're headed in to town," Britt said mockingly when they reached the chairs. She sighed deeply as she dropped into one. "Said they are on a wine crawl."

"You mean they aren't done for the day?" Amelia laughed.

Britt just raised her eyebrows. "So if you're looking for a good time, you know where to go. And if you're looking for some peace and quiet, you know what to avoid."

"Chances are Jackson will find them before the day is through," Robbie laughed, and Matt joined in.

Amelia sipped her wine and waited to see if Matt would make an excuse, leave, or mention his plans for the evening. He was staying with Jackson, after all. And Jackson often took Sunday evenings off if he had someone to cover the bar.

Amelia knew this because that's how life in Blue Harbor was. You knew everything about everyone, for the most part, and what wasn't directly told would all too soon be revealed.

She wondered if Robbie knew any more details of Matt's plans than she did. She supposed he did. And if so, perhaps he'd shared them with Britt. She made a mental note to ask her sister when she had her alone. Discreetly, of course. She didn't need her sister pushing her to get back together with Matt like Gabby had. It wasn't that straightforward. And Amelia knew that life didn't always work out the way you wished it would.

"You going over to Dad's tonight?" Britt asked her.

Amelia hesitated. Before Candy came along, she'd spent most of her nights off with their father, and sometimes Cora or Maddie had joined. Now, she didn't feel quite so needed anymore. It was both liberating and a little depressing.

"I saw him the other night at the café," Amelia said. "Besides, this is my busy season. Better make the most of it while I can."

"I hope today helped," Britt said. She understood just how seasonal work could be in a small, lakefront town like Blue Harbor, and Amelia was fully aware that Britt was hard at work strategizing how to get through the long, cold, winter without seeing a dip in the orchard's profits.

"It did," Amelia said. And it had been worth the extra effort, too. Especially since Matt had decided to stop by. "And I agree with Robbie and your ideas earlier too. We should do this again, Britt. It's a great way to show off the orchard, and I have to admit that I didn't mind the paycheck."

"That makes two of us!" Britt remarked. To Matt she said, "I'm still trying to figure out a plan for the winter. My father used that as a break, but I think there is something to offer here, and maybe a reason to pull people into town, even for just a weekend."

"Did you have anything specific in mind?"

Amelia laughed. "When doesn't Britt have something in mind?"

"Guilty as charged," Britt said, grinning. "I'm always coming up with new ideas for this place. It's just so full of possibility, you know?"

Amelia knew. It was how she felt when she first took the keys over for the café. She could still remember the wonder of standing in the center of the room, staring at the counter and the tables and the windows, and knowing that it was all hers and she could do whatever she wanted with it.

Robbie leaned forward. "What about your ideas, Matt? You keep hinting at a reason to be in town. Are you ever going to tell us what you're hatching?"

"Well, I shouldn't give too many details away," Matt said, but from the tone, he intended to do just that. "But I happen to think that if the project I'm pitching goes through, you will all see an increase in tourist activity around here. Year-round."

Amelia caught the excitement in Britt's eyes and sat a little straighter. "Really? What are you planning exactly?"

"A five-star waterfront resort," Matt said.

Amelia frowned. Most of the accommodations in town were small and mid-sized inns, each old and passed down through the generations, most of them similar in appearance: white with black shutters. Several, like the Carriage House Inn, lined Main Street and farther around the coastline, several larger ones faced the water. But none of them were a resort. A resort meant amenities, and land to accommodate it.

"You really think it would work in a town like this? There's not a lot to do," she pointed out, but it was Britt who cut in excitedly.

"Relaxation would be the big sell!" She grinned at Matt. "I think it's just what the area needs. A high-end option for a whole new set of tourists. You could offer water activities. Boat rentals. Oh, I assume there will be a spa."

And probably a café, too. Or a restaurant. Maybe more than one. Amelia struggled to see how that would be good for business, but then, the customers who were attracted to such luxurious accommodations probably wouldn't have much interest in her little café with the scuffed floorboards and the mismatched tables and the patio chairs that she'd painted pink and yellow as a contrast to the surrounding blue of the water and green from the trees.

"I'm just the architect, but the developer I work for would determine what amenities to include based on demographic pull and space use, of course. But I definitely think it could work. In fact, I think it could make Blue Harbor even better than it was before."

Amelia wished she could feel more excited about this, but the thought of a huge new building in town made her uneasy.

"You don't look convinced," Matt said, looking a little concerned.

"I am," she explained. "I mean, I'm sure it would be a big draw for tourists. But..." She shrugged. "I guess I like Blue Harbor just as it is."

"Now you sound like Dad!" Britt scolded, but she waggled her finger in a mocking way. It was not lost on the four Conway daughters that their father didn't like change—that was, until he surprised them by falling for Candy, and then promptly handing over the business he'd run for all of his adult life to Britt. He hadn't even batted an eyelash when she immediately started making changes to his well-established ways—and that had been a surprise to everyone.

She pulled in a breath. Maybe change was good. It could bring Matt back to town, couldn't it?

Olivia Miles

"It's not all the same," Robbie pointed out. "When I moved back I saw the changes. Good ones. Ones that remained true to the town. You had taken over the café, for starters. And Gabby has the flower shop."

Amelia considered this. Gabby's cousin on her mother's side had Bella's Books. A new generation had taken over, but the heart of Blue Harbor remained.

Fortunately, Matt had always loved the town's charm every bit as much as she did.

"Maybe you can show me around?" Matt grinned at her. "Re-acquaint me with the town?"

Amelia knew from the burn of her cheeks that Robbie and Britt were watching this all with great amusement. Easy for them, when they'd settled into a happy relationship once again.

She swallowed hard and took another sip of her cool drink. Liquid courage. "I have Mondays off."

"Tomorrow works," Matt said. His gaze lingered long enough for her stomach to tighten, his eyes intense, and his smile pulling right at her heartstrings. "Looking forward to it."

She bit down on her lip. So was she. Even if it meant she might have to try to squeeze that manicure appointment in tonight, if possible.

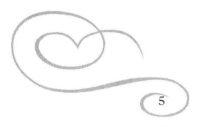

5

The only salon in all of Blue Harbor was located in the heart of town on Pine Street. It was a popular destination for most residents, including Amelia's cousins. Amelia's own mother had come here, back when it was still owned by Nina Payne's mother, but Amelia had only been once: for her junior prom.

She smiled at the memory as she approached the storefront. She'd gone to the dance with Matt, of course. Worn a blue dress and had her hair styled into some elaborate up-do that she'd seen in a magazine. Her father had insisted, as a treat, his eyes shining with tears that her mother couldn't be there to see her, looking so beautiful.

Amelia had felt guilty, but her father was right. It had been a treat. And a distraction. The Conway girls usually trimmed each other's hair, Amelia taking over the task that their mother had once provided in the master bathroom every two months. No frills, no real style, just a good cutting of the split ends.

The first time Amelia had taken the shears to Cora's auburn locks, she'd been sixteen, and despite observing her mother's method over the years, she'd managed to give Cora a lopsided cut that had resulted in so much trimming to balance it out, that in the end she'd taken more than three inches off and both sisters were in tears.

Cora had fared no better when it was her turn to help Amelia, and the raucous had prompted their father to stand in the hallway thrusting cash into their hands, begging them to go into town for a proper haircut!

But going into town for a real haircut meant more change. And it was a bitter reminder that not only was their mother gone, but so were the comfortable ways of their life that they'd depended on, and cherished, even when they hadn't known it. They'd pressed on, been more careful the next time, and even though they didn't all live together in the old Victorian waterfront home anymore, they still called on each other whenever they needed to, and jumped at the chance to lend a hand.

Nina was standing at the counter when Amelia walked in, hoping they might have time to squeeze her in before the close of business. Nina had been a few years ahead of Amelia in school, and she'd taken over the business from her mother a few years back. When they were kids, she always had the newest styles, was the first in her grade to wear makeup, and explained how to properly apply mascara to a large number of girls in the gymnasium locker room one day after recess. Now, she had softened her look over the years, but it was clear that she took pride in her appearance.

Whereas Amelia...she could only hope that her mother had not just been doting when she claimed her to be a natural beauty.

"You're in luck!" Nina said with a big smile. "We're wrapping up one other client, so we can fit you right in. Mani or pedi?"

Seeing as it was summer, and she *did* have a quasi-date tomorrow, Amelia said, "Both."

Amelia breathed a sigh of relief, feeling giddy at the thought of doing something as indulgent as getting her nails painted when she had perfectly good polish at home given to her as a stocking stuffer last Christmas and her manicure was bound to chip an hour into service on Tuesday, but she had to admit, this was fun.

"Actually, do you have room for one more? I'll text my sister." Cora would be closing up her holiday shop by now, because tourists who came to Blue Harbor did buy from her store year-round.

Nina nodded. "Sure thing. I'll get the water going."

The water! Amelia fired off a text to Cora and received a quick reply that she'd be there in five minutes. The convenience of small town living never grew old. While she waited, Amelia eased herself into the massage chair and relaxed her neck against the headrest, closing her eyes as her feet soaked in the bubbling, warm water.

Really, she should do this more often. At least, when time and funds allowed for it.

She was nearly about to nod off when she was startled by the sound of a long, low groan. She looked around, for the sound of a cat in distress, or perhaps some strange backwind from the air-conditioning unit—but then the sound came again, louder this time, and she looked over in horror to see a woman two chairs down having her feet rubbed with a pink sugar scrub.

The woman groaned again, louder this time, and Amelia's eyes opened in alarm. It wasn't just any woman. It was—

The woman pulled the magazine that had been shielding her face down onto her lap and let out a purr.

"Oh, that's *wonderful*. Yes, right there. Thank you, love."

"Candy?" Amelia's mouth was dry.

Candy jerked her head toward her, her eyes lighting up with excitement. "Amelia! Did you just come in? And oh, you're getting a pedicure too! We can make a girls day of it!"

Amelia felt her smile slip. "Cora's on her way."

She wondered if she should send her sister another text, warning her or telling her not to come, but then she thought that no, she needed backup here, and quick.

Candy clasped her hands together. "Perfect! The more the merrier, I always say! Merrier! Get it?"

Amelia smiled politely at the joke no doubt referring to Cora's holiday shop.

Normally, Amelia might say the same. That more *was* better, especially when it meant all of her sisters or cousins were together, but not in this case. Not when she was looking for a little time to pamper herself—quietly. And to think...about this afternoon. And what tomorrow could bring. Her stomach tensed with anticipation at the thought of seeing Matt again. Being alone. Spending a day together.

She glanced at Candy, forcing herself not to get too ahead of her rational thoughts. Maybe Candy being here was for the best.

"I thought you'd be home with Dad and Maddie," Amelia said. Once, Sunday nights were reserved for traditional family dinners, and Amelia had even kept that going when she'd opened the café. It was one of the reasons that they closed early on Sundays. But with her father's injury and Candy's arrival, a lot had changed.

"I like to pamper myself on Sundays," Candy said matter-of-factly. "It's important to start the week off right."

Note to self, Amelia thought. She noticed that Candy was peering at her most intensely.

"Who does your hair, dear?"

Amelia ran a self-conscious hand through her hair that was still pulled back in a ponytail from today's event. "Oh, Cora usually trims it."

Candy's eyes burst open. "Cora!"

Amelia shrugged. "It's just a trim. It's not like I need anything fancy." Still she heard the defensive edge creep into her tone.

Now Candy's eyes were practically bulging. The woman attempting to now paint her toenails gave her a look of impatience as she guided her foot back onto the towel.

"You don't need anything fancy?" Candy repeated. "Of course you do! You're a woman! And a young and attractive one!"

Once again, Amelia thought back to Gabby's words yesterday. Maybe she was a little too practical for her own good.

"I wear my hair up in a ponytail for work most days, anyway, Candy." Amelia gave a little shrug, hoping to close down the topic, but Candy was on a mission, and given the life force that she was, Amelia knew that there was no escaping her now.

"I'll let you in on a little secret," Candy said, lowering her voice to a loud whisper, even though they were the only clients in the salon and Amelia would put money on every person on staff already being privy to whatever Candy was about to reveal. "This is not my natural hair color."

Candy pressed a finger to her lips and waited for a reaction. The only sound to be heard was a snort of laughter from Nina, who quickly smothered it with a cough when Candy shot her a look of disapproval. She went back to straightening shampoo bottles, her shoulders shaking.

Amelia swallowed hard. It was no shock that Candy's blond hair was not the color she was born with—her eyebrows made that much clear. Still, she did her best to play along. "Wow. It looks really nice, Candy."

Candy beamed and patted her curls. "It does, doesn't it? And it's all thanks to these two ladies. They are amazing colorists."

"Well now, Candy, I did advise on a darker shade—" Nina cut in, but Candy just brushed her hand through the air.

"Pfft. A woman can never be too blond, and a man can..." She gave a coy grin. "Well, never you mind. I don't think I need to spell that out, do I?" She laughed loudly, and snorted at the end, just as the bell above the door rang and Cora entered, looking so bewildered that Amelia now felt guilty for not warning her away.

"Cora!" Candy trilled. She patted the seat between herself and Amelia with force. "We're having a girls' day! Come sit and dish."

Amelia studied her hands as Cora obeyed. Still, she knew there would be hell to pay for this later.

"So tell me everything. Who are you dating? Who do you have your eye on?"

Cora slanted a glare in Amelia's direction. "Not much to tell, Candy," she sighed. "I haven't dated much."

Candy clucked her tongue. "Before I met your father, I dated several men. You have to kiss a lot of toads, sometimes."

Amelia and Cora nodded. Amelia said a silent prayer that Candy wouldn't be going into any details.

"Take this one guy, for example," Candy said, and Amelia sucked in a breath, bracing herself. "Do you know that man could spit a cherry pit clear across the kitchen, and have it land right in the garbage can?"

Not sure if Candy thought this was a virtue or not, Amelia laughed uneasily. "My!"

The woman at Candy's feet gave her leg a little jerk, reminding Candy to stop squirming. Candy ignored her and twisted her body farther to face the sisters, eager to continue her story.

"I finally said, Roy, do you even like cherries or do you just like spitting their pits?"

Amelia tittered politely. "Pretty ironic that you ended up with my father, then. The cherries on our orchard are practically a bigger draw than the winery!"

Candy smiled serenely as she set her hands in her lap. "Some things are just meant to be. It's like the universe is trying to tell you something, you know?"

Amelia didn't know, nor did she want to know, and she nearly kicked Cora when she said, "And what was the universe telling you, Candy?"

"Well, it didn't directly say anything, obviously." Candy honked in laughter. "But it was almost like it was hinting at me. Cherries. Cherries," she chanted.

Amelia picked up the nearest magazine, even if it was for senior citizens, and brought it to her face to cover the laughter she could no longer hold back.

"It's upside down," Cora hissed.

Was it? Damn. It was. Amelia did her best to compose herself before setting it back. "Sorry. Just...thought I was going to cough."

Cora narrowed her gaze. Candy didn't seem to notice. "Well, enough about my love life. Cora, I was just telling Amelia that she should go for a cut and highlight." Candy gave Amelia a very pointed look. "I happened to see a *very* good looking young man enter the kitchen of the café the other night."

Cora widened her eyes on Amelia. "Oh?"

*Not her too*, Amelia thought with annoyance.

"Robbie's cousin," Candy informed Cora.

Now Cora looked downright shocked. Being holed up in her holiday shop in August wasn't the best place to find out the latest happenings in town.

"Matt *Bradford*?" Cora gaped. "Matt is back in town?"

Amelia pursed her lips and reached for another magazine. "Apparently so."

"Handsome devil," Candy stage-whispered.

Amelia didn't reply to that, because it was true. The man was handsome. Always had been.

"I must say that it's rather...*encouraging* to see Amelia tending to her appearance." Candy waggled her eyebrows as if she were in on some secret. "But then she told me that you've been cutting her hair all these years!"

Cora just shrugged. "We cut each other's hair."

Candy opened her mouth—widely, and for an extended period of time.

"Well, now I've heard it all. You girls cutting each other's hair! Last I checked, none of you were a professional at it."

"It's fine," Amelia said, her tone a little stronger this time. "We both like our hair all one length. Besides, Cora has wonderful natural highlights."

They both did, really, not that she was one to draw attention to herself. They'd both inherited

their father's hair, which pulled lovely copper strands by midsummer.

Candy gripped the top of Cora's head and gave it a turn, giving a little mew of approval at what she saw.

"Well, if you do decide to go a shade lighter, I'll share my color with you. But just remember. Our secret!"

Cora shifted her eyes over to Amelia who this time decided it was officially time to bury herself in a magazine. She could reach for one of the cooking options—they were usually her favorite, and she never tired of new ideas for the menu at the café. But today, she reached for a fashion magazine. If things were going to start changing in Blue Harbor, she supposed it was high time that she made a few improvements, too!

*

Jackson lived in a small house at the far end of town, on the waterfront, with his own private dock, a fishing boat that had seen better days and probably wasn't safe to take out, and hidden by dense pine trees.

"For someone as social as you, I'm surprised you don't go stir crazy out here," Matt remarked. Growing up, Jackson was always initiating some fun on the evenings and weekends, wanting to get out and be where the action was. And from the looks of things, not much had changed. Jackson was charming, and boisterous, and he wasn't shy in making it known that, unlike his younger brother, he wasn't looking to settle down anytime soon. He liked his fun, and his flirting.

But then, Matt supposed he had enough of that at his job at the inn. And there was something to be said for the quiet surroundings, away from distraction or temptation. It gave you a chance to think. Or not think. To just be.

He pulled in a breath. His mind had been on overdrive for so long he couldn't remember the last time he had sat and listened to nature. Probably not since he left town in the first place.

They were sitting on the deck, nursing beers, and looking out over the moonlit water. It was just the kind of view that the guests of the new resort would be taking in if his plans went through. He made a mental note to snap photos of it for his upcoming presentation. The view alone could sway someone's decision, as would all this solitude. Even though the spot he'd targeted was at the opposite edge of town, he knew that it would have a similar feel. Dense forest, clear water, and a sky as big as the Milky Way itself.

"I like the balance," Jackson said with a shrug. "Besides, there's a reason I'm still single. Dating is one thing, but I like my alone time."

"And here I just thought you hadn't found a girl willing to put up with you for the long haul," Matt bantered.

"Very funny." Jackson shook his head. "What about you? Seeing anyone?"

Matt took a sip of his beer. "I was for a while. We broke up a couple of months back."

"What went wrong?"

"Nothing went wrong," Matt said slowly. "It was more that it never really felt right." Really, none of the so-called relationships he'd had since leaving Blue Harbor had felt right. They'd been short-lived, some fun, others forced, and they had all ended without much regret or reflection.

Unlike his time with Amelia. She was the one girl he still thought about, all these years later.

"She wanted to get married," Matt explained.

Jackson rolled his eyes. "They all do! That's why I don't stick around long enough for them to start getting any ideas."

Matt laughed. "I'm not opposed to marriage. I just didn't see myself marrying her, honestly." He felt bad about it. Still did. But being back here, around Amelia...it reminded him that he'd made the right decision. There was something natural about being with her, something that didn't feel forced or over thought, even now, after all these years.

"You're looking to settle down?" Jackson's tone held a note of surprise.

Matt hadn't really thought of it like that, but now he shrugged. "Right now I'm focused on my career, but I'm not eliminating the possibility of a personal life. With the right woman, of course."

"And what about Amelia?"

Matt tried to cover the tension that the mere mention of her name triggered by taking another sip of his beer, only to find it empty. He reached forward and grabbed another from the cooler that Jackson kept outside, and popped off the cap.

"What about her?"

Jackson cut him a knowing look. "Don't be coy, Matt. You were crazy about each other once."

"Once." Matt drank back a long sip. "But that was a long time ago. I'm sure she's moved on."

He couldn't deny the interest that stirred when Jackson shook his head. "Nope. Not really. She spent so much time taking care of her sisters and her father that I'm not sure it left much time for anything else. Well, other than her café."

Now Matt shifted in his chair. "So she owns that café?"

Jackson nodded. "Bought it from Dorothy in a private sale over five years back. I don't think she was asking for much. Just happy to have someone to pass it along to."

"Bad business," Matt muttered.

Jackson gave him a quizzical smile. "It's a small town. That's the kind of stuff that people do in a community. It's not always about dollars and cents."

Only sometimes it was, Matt thought, thinking of how much all that did matter when it was suddenly gone. His father's business had struggled for years, until he'd mortgaged the house to the hilt in an attempt to keep it going. The community couldn't save him then, could they?

He pulled in a breath, not wanting to bother with an argument, or pointing out how different his circumstances were to Jackson's.

Matt fell silent as he sipped his beer and looked out over the water. From this view, he could see the twinkling lights of the larger resorts on Evening Island—the types of places with restaurants and pools and golfing. Things that Blue Harbor lacked.

But not for long.

"Anyway," he said firmly. "I'm in town for business, really." And he needed to remind himself of that, even if seeing Amelia again was a perk. Without the resort, though, there was nothing for him here other than bad memories and a feeling in his gut that he just couldn't shake.

"You're really excited about this project," Jackson commented.

Matt nodded. "I am." More than anyone could ever understand, especially his cousins. They'd been able to stay. Their parents had a stable business. Jackson or Robbie could someday take it over if they wished, and chances were that Jackson someday would.

Whereas Matt... Matt had to leave all this behind. The view. The sky. The friends. The family.

And now, it was all within reach again. If he could just make sure that resort was built.

6

The next morning, Amelia took her time inspecting her closet, even though she didn't exactly love anything she saw. With great reluctance, she went down the steps that led from her deck to the patio and tapped on the door of Maddie's garden unit apartment. She glanced at the vegetable garden while she waited, knowing that she'd have to pick some of those tomatoes before they over-ripened. She'd put a tomato and mozzarella salad on the menu for tomorrow night. The basil plant that sat on her kitchen window ledge was due for a clipping.

Still, when the door opened, she quickly forgot all about the café. She was here on a mission. And she suddenly felt like it wasn't one she could see through.

Opening a business? That was easy. But putting yourself out there—emotionally—that was something different. Foreign. And a little scary.

"Can I borrow something to wear for the day?" She didn't know why she was ringing her hands. It was a normal thing for sisters to do, after all. Cora and Maddie used to swap clothes all the time growing up. It was just not normal for her.

Sure enough, Maddie looked at her suspiciously. "You don't have any clean clothes? But you always do laundry on Sundays."

True, she usually did, except that last night she'd been too busy being pampered at the salon.

"I was hoping to try on that yellow sundress you wore recently. The one with the scoop neck?"

Now Maddie's expression changed to one of interest. "To grocery shop and make menu lists?" she asked, referring to Amelia's typical Monday routine.

Amelia should have known her sister wouldn't make this easy for her. She sighed. "Fine. If you must know, I'm spending part of the day showing Matt around town."

"Showing him around town? But he lived here for the first eighteen years of his life."

"And he hasn't been back in twelve," Amelia said. When it came out like that, she realized just how much time had passed—how much life had been lived, how many experiences had happened. Not that she'd had many. The days had rolled along, peacefully enough, but she couldn't really pinpoint anything exciting that had happened other than opening her café.

Her pride and joy.

"I'm going to be working when I'm done," Amelia said. She did need to get work done, and while the café may be closed to the public on Mondays, she was never off duty.

"And what if Matt invites you to dinner? And then dinner turns into drinks? And then drinks turn into..." Maddie waggled her eyebrows, and Amelia sighed heavily, pushing past her into the small hallway of Maddie's apartment that together they had painted the softest shade of blue. She was officially calling upon her role as Landlady now.

"The dress is in my closet and you are free to borrow it," Maddie said.

Amelia smiled at her, thankful that this little game was now over. "Thank you."

But from the gleam in Maddie's eyes, she wasn't quite finished yet. Her lips twisted into a coy grin as she leaned against the doorjamb to her bedroom, blocking Amelia's entry.

"If."

Amelia stared at her. "If?"

"If you promise to come back here and tell me everything that happened when you return the dress."

Considering that Maddie was bound to drag every last detail from her regardless, Amelia saw no point in refusing.

"You have a deal. I'll tell you every last juicy tidbit."

Not that she expected there to be any. Really, she didn't know what to expect. And that was very nerve-racking.

She left Maddie's apartment with the dress in hand and hurried back upstairs in time to change and pull her hair back into a ponytail. Then, thinking the better of it, she pulled out the elastic band and let her hair fall loose at her shoulders.

Before she could over think it further, she grabbed her canvas tote, slipped into some comfortable sandals that showed off her freshly painted pink toenails, and walked to the front door with a pounding heart.

Matt was standing at the base of her steps when she stepped outside, feeling harried and flushed, even though it was early still and the breeze off the lake was cool.

"Hey, you," he said, jamming his hands into the pockets of his khaki shorts. He was standing beside a bicycle that he had clearly rented in town—the aqua blue color was a dead giveaway. "It's a nice day. You up for a ride?"

Amelia was happy that the yellow sundress had a full enough skirt, so she wouldn't have to change into something from her closet—or worse—knock on Maddie's door again.

She glanced back at Maddie's windows as she walked toward the bike rack at the side of the

house, just in time to see the curtains quickly pulled shut.

She grinned wryly. Really! Was it such a big deal that she had a date today?

Sadly, it was. And sadly, this may not be a date at all. It was just two old friends. Going for a ride.

"I brought us breakfast," Matt said, picking up a bag from the front basket of his bike.

Amelia laughed. "I don't think I've had someone else cook me breakfast in—" In longer than she should admit, especially to an old boyfriend. Yes, she might run her own café, and she might cook better than most people in this town, but she didn't need to reveal how seldom it was that a guy came along and did something nice for her, and no, she didn't think her father counted.

"Oh, I didn't cook anything," Matt clarified. He opened the bag to reveal an assortment of bagels and a few containers of cream cheese. "Jackson buys these by the dozen at that deli over in Pine Falls. I didn't think he'd notice if a few were missing."

She laughed. "I love bagels. And I haven't been to Pine Falls in forever." It was where Candy had grown up, just the next town south, and Amelia realized just how insular her world had become. How she'd accepted a long time ago that Blue Harbor was where she was needed and where she would remain.

She looked at Matt. His hair was tousled, rustling in the breeze, and his eyes were warm and kind and as blue as the lake water. She'd stopped thinking about what she was missing. Until now.

"Maybe we could stop down near the waterfront? Have a little picnic? I'd suggest we grab coffee along the way, but I believe your café is closed." His grin made her heart pick up speed.

"The grocery store sells coffee," Amelia reminded him. It might not be as good as what she made, but it would do. Besides, for once, she didn't care how her coffee tasted. She just cared that she was here, with Matt, and that she hadn't felt this alive since she was a kid.

They rode along the path toward Main Street, which was quieter than it had been just twenty-four hours ago, with the weekend crowd now gone, and parked their bikes there. Cathy, the shopkeeper, was used to seeing her on Mondays for the odds and ends she didn't pick up from local farms or order in bulk. She called over to her, but Amelia just smiled and said, "Actually, we're just stopping by for coffee. "

We. It sounded nice on her lips.

She glanced at Matt to see if he was bothered by the term, but he just reached for a paper cup and filled it from one of the carafes that lined the counter near the front of the store.

Cathy looked from her to Matt in obvious surprise. "Matt Bradford. Nice to see you back in town! Tell me, how are your parents?"

Matt's smile seemed to slip for a moment. "Just fine. My brother too. Thanks for asking."

"I'll be back again later for my usual order," Amelia told Cathy, while Matt settled the bill. Cathy gave her a wink of approval as Amelia walked to the door.

"How *are* your parents, by the way?" It hadn't come up before, and Amelia felt bad now for not asking sooner. She'd always loved his mother—a generous woman with a big laugh and a kind smile, who had dropped off a casserole each week for a month after Amelia's mother had passed away. And his father was quiet but thoughtful, always greeting her with a smile, and telling her to come by the shop sometime.

Matt kept his eyes ahead and took a sip of his coffee. "They're fine." He looked over at her and shrugged, as if there was nothing more to say.

Amelia let it drop, and they walked down to the green stretch of grass that led to the lakefront, before settling on a picnic table near the docks.

"So, I take it you usually work on Mondays?" Matt asked, once they were seated. "I hope I didn't keep you from anything."

"Not at all. I do work a lot, and Mondays are catch-up days. It's nice to take some time off when I can."

"Work keeps you too busy for fun?" He looked at her across the table as he pulled a bagel from the bag and passed it to her. By fun, did he mean dating?

She shrugged. "Something like that. Work and family. Although, now my dad has a girlfriend, so…"

"That's an adjustment, I imagine." Matt's eyes were kind as he studied her, and against her will, Amelia felt a lump build up in her throat. Her mother had been gone since she was sixteen, and she should be used to it by now, except that she wasn't. None of them were. And Matt knew that. Because he'd known her. How special she was. How warm and funny. He'd been there when she was here, and he'd been there when she was gone.

But then he was gone, too.

Amelia sighed and used a plastic knife to spread the cream cheese over a bagel half. "An adjustment, yes. She's nothing like my mother, which might be a blessing in disguise, I suppose."

"No one could compare with your mother," Matt said quietly.

Her eyes burned as she continued to spread the already spread cream cheese. She pursed her lips and slanted him a glance. "Her name is Candy."

Matt laughed, and it was just what she needed to break up the moment. "Well that's a change."

She nodded. "Change is inevitable, I suppose."

But sitting here, across from the one boy she had ever loved, she didn't feel like much had changed at all.

"So, tell me more about this project you're so excited about," she said, biting into her bagel.

"You didn't sound so enthusiastic about it yesterday," Matt said.

"If it keeps you around a little longer, how can I not support it?"

He grinned at her until his eyes crinkled at the corners and her cheeks burned. Good grief, she was flirting! It had been years since she had flirted, or even had occasion to try it! But it felt good. And fun. And...right.

Matt set down his bagel and reached into his pocket for his phone. "Okay then. You asked for it."

He slid the device across the table, revealing a giant, white...box.

"*That's* the hotel you designed?" She couldn't hide her shock, and when she met his eyes, she realized that her reaction wasn't the one he'd been looking for. Struggling to find something polite to say, she said, "It's just...so modern. So...sleek."

So cold. So sterile.

"Thank you," Matt said, but there was a hint of question in his tone. "I think."

"No, I mean it." Amelia swallowed hard and pushed a strand of hair behind her ears, buying time as she studied the photo. Was that...an entire wall of glass? There wasn't a window pane to be found. The entire building was concrete. The only things made of concrete in Blue Harbor were the sidewalks and building foundations.

"It's just...so different than what you usually see around here."

Matt nodded. "Exactly. It's fresh. It's new. It's what this town needs."

Now he had officially managed to surprise her. "What this town needs?" She stared at him in disbelief. Was this what he really thought?

"This town is old—"

"This town is charming," she corrected, feeling defensive of the place she still called home. "It's the old-world style that is so appealing. People have sky scrapers in the city. The tourists come here because they like how quaint it is."

"Enough tourists?" Matt raised an eyebrow.

"Enough," Amelia said, but she knew her tone was far from convincing. "Look, the winters are always slow—"

"But they don't have to be," Matt insisted. He was tapping at something on the photo, but Amelia couldn't bear the thought of looking at it anymore.

"This resort has a full spa, heated terraces, winter sports—"

"And you think that this sort of hotel will attract more business than the inns on Main Street or the bigger places along the beachfront?"

"None of those places have full amenities. One might have a pool, but then it doesn't have a restaurant, and vice versa. And it won't take business away from the existing businesses. It will add business. The tourists who come here are looking for a getaway and they'll be willing to pay a premium for it. Trust me, Amelia, it will be the best thing that ever happened to the economy, and you as a business owner should see that."

"I don't doubt that, and I agree that there's certainly enough demand for more hotel rooms. But..."

His eyes challenged hers and he thrust the phone back into his pocket. "But? Go on. Say it."

She sighed, hating that this perfect morning was already veering off course.

"I still think that the people who come to Blue Harbor are looking for a quaint, small-town experience. The big resorts on Evening Island do well and they're definitely from a different era."

"The big resorts on Evening Island are our competition, and we'd need to set ourselves apart." Matt shook his head. "Besides, when the ferries stop running in the winter, those places close down. All those customers could end up right here. In Blue Harbor."

"But...you used to love the old charm of this town." It was true. He loved the Colonial architecture of the buildings, the fact that Main Street was a step back in time. "Remember how your father taught you the history of the town? He loved collecting old furniture and artwork that dated as far back as the founders!"

Matt's eyes went flat. "And where did that get him? No one wanted to buy that old stuff. They didn't appreciate it like he did. Sure, they'd poke around, but did anyone really buy anything? No."

Amelia nodded sadly. There was no way to change his mind in this conversation, it would seem.

Except that maybe...maybe she could show him something that would open his mind, or at least remind him of what made this town so special to begin with—and not just for the tourists.

"Let me show you something," she said, packing up the empty paper bag and tossing it in the nearby trash. "I promise, it will be worth it." She grinned, trying to lessen the tension, and after a moment, Matt did too.

Still, her heart felt heavy as they walked back up to Main Street and she climbed onto her bike. These shops and storefronts and inns were what made this town what it was—what set it apart from the suburbs of bigger cities. What made it a destination for some and a home for others, like herself.

It all felt like it was slipping away, right along with the possibility that she and Matt might find something between them again. Nothing about this day was going as planned. Or rather, as hoped.

She led him down familiar roads, roads that she had travelled on so many afternoons after school and on weekends, until they finally turned onto the street where Matt used to live. She stopped outside the old Victorian home, with the gables and front porch that were much like her own childhood home in many ways, and just as familiar.

"It's for sale!" Matt exclaimed, noting the sign in the front yard.

She nodded. "The people who moved in after you just moved a couple months ago."

Matt parked his bike on the front path and walked up onto the porch, peering in windows and trying the door.

"We can probably get in," Amelia offered, as she brushed her toe over her kickstand to put it down and left her bike beside Matt's. "Lanie Thompson is a real estate agent now and she's a regular at the café." Egg white frittata for breakfast, kale salad for dinner, dressing on the side. Like Amelia, she was still single, but unlike Amelia she made time for various work out classes, beauty routines, and...diets. "I bet if we call her, she'll give us the code for the lock."

Matt seemed to hesitate, but Amelia sensed that he wanted to go back inside. And he needed to see it. To remember how much he loved it, and not just because it was home, but because the architecture of the old house was what had inspired him in the first place—much more so than that great modern thing he had shown her earlier.

Without waiting for a reply, she went back to her bike and pulled her phone from the tote that was resting in the wire basket. Less than a minute later, the code to the key lock had been texted and they were opening the door into the house.

"They painted," Matt said when they stepped inside the front hallway, which used to be cluttered with shoes and raincoats and umbrellas and baseball bats and mitts and Matt's lacrosse stick, resting against the wall near the coat rack.

Amelia pushed back a wave of nostalgia and looked around. He was right. The house had been darker before, and now the woodwork was white, and airy. She rather liked it.

"It looks better," Matt said, standing planted to the floor.

"I'm sure it feels different now," Amelia said. "After all this time. But it's still a great house."

Matt nodded as he stepped into the living room. "It always was," he said quietly. "It was the best."

*

Matt walked through each of the empty rooms, remembering them as they once were. There, in the corner of the kitchen, near the big bay window that looked out onto the shady yard, was where he used to sit and eat his waffles and eggs each morning and do his homework each afternoon. The cabinets were still old, but the ceilings were high, and the windows, while in need of some repair, were original, and exquisite, especially, he thought as he came back into the hallway, the stained-glass oval on the landing of the stairs.

He let out a breath as he moved his hand up the carved wood banister, so much different than the sleek metal he now opted for in all of his designs. The door handles were glass, carved knobs, with a brass center, and at the back of the upstairs hall was his childhood bedroom, not that he could say it was his favorite room in the house.

No, his favorite room had been the dining room, and the parlor, with their French doors and heavy woodwork and the oversized windows from which his mother hung long paneled draped that went all the way to the ceiling. And the ceilings! He'd nearly forgotten the details of those rooms, with their layered and intricate crown moldings.

He walked through the house slowly, filled with sounds and voices and memories so clear that it cut straight through him, and he wondered more than once if he should have stayed outside, because it had been tempting to do just that.

But it had been more tempting to come inside.

He studied the fireplace—the carved detail of the mantle, where his mother used to hang their stockings. And there, in the bay window of the parlor was where their Christmas tree had always stood.

And where he had sat, on the window seat, staring at the rooms that sprawled off the hallway, as the movers carried their belongings to the truck waiting outside, until the house was no longer home, and could never be put back together as it once was.

"You loved this house," Amelia said softly. "I did too."

"A shame to see it empty like this," he said, shifting uncomfortably on his feet. This house was meant to be filled—with furniture and laughter.

He glanced at Amelia. It was meant to be filled with love.

Amelia just shrugged. "Oh, I'm sure that someone will buy it soon enough. They don't make houses like this anymore."

He shook his head. "No. They don't."

It had good bones. It was sturdy. But more than that, it was special and unique, each turn gave a new surprise, and no detail went unnoticed.

"I wonder..." Amelia said. She looked at him expectantly. "Do you think they kept the old swing?"

A slow realization built as the memories came back. Long summer nights and cool autumn afternoons, side by side on the old swing that hung from the rafters of the back porch.

He hadn't thought of that swing in at least ten years—maybe more. It was easier sometimes, to harden his heart to this town, rather than look back fondly on it, and hold on too close. But it was also impossible to fully do so. His happiest memories were in this town. And many of them were with the woman now standing before him, her eyes bright, her smile still beautiful.

"We could check," he offered, even as he braced himself for the inevitable disappointment he would feel if it were gone. Heck, it had been creaky back when he lived here.

Slowly, they moved to the kitchen again, and Amelia pushed through the screen door, the smile she tossed over her shoulder nearly as big as the relief he felt. And sure enough, there it was, the paint still chipped, and chains still squeaky.

"Do you think it's safe to sit on?" Amelia stood back, looking wary.

"Only one way to find out," Matt said, dropping himself onto the swing, bouncing a few times. He looked up at the porch ceiling, which showed no signs of rot or disrepair. "Seems sturdy to me."

He patted the seat beside him and didn't even scoot over when she sat beside him, stirring up a desire he was struggling to fight. She smelled sweet—but it wasn't perfume or any specific effort on her part, he knew. It was a familiar scent, something that brought him back to another time. Something that brought him home.

"I hope it was okay, coming here," she said, turning to give him a hesitant smile.

He nodded, looking out over the yard. At the tree he and his brother used to climb. At the basketball hoop still attached the top of the detached garage.

"In many ways it feels like yesterday," he commented. "In other ways, it feels like I never left."

They locked eyes for a moment before she looked away, blushing.

"One of my biggest regrets in life was leaving this town," he said. It felt strange, saying it aloud, but he'd always been able to talk to Amelia. Deep down, he still felt he could, that there connection was still there.

"Then why didn't you ever visit? You could have come for the summer—"

He shook his head, shutting that down. "It wasn't that simple. I had a summer job, to help the family and help with college. And I worked all through college, too. And..." He bit back the emotions building inside him. "And it wouldn't have been the same."

She nodded slowly, scuffing her sandals against the porch floor. "I understand. It's not your home anymore."

Matt looked around the yard and the porch and back up to the house behind him. If he wanted to, he could almost dare to pretend that it wasn't empty and painted inside, but that it was just as it had once been. When it had been his.

"No, it's not," he said gruffly, shaking himself out of all these sentimental feelings. He'd grown. He'd changed. He wasn't the boy who lived here, and he hadn't been for some time. This place might have inspired him, but it had changed him too.

"But you do see the beauty in it?" Her eyes seemed to plead with his. "You loved this house. You loved the charm. The details."

He shook his head. "That was a long time ago, Amelia. I'm a different person now."

"But—"

"But this house represents the past. In every possible way." His jaw tightened and he saw her open her mouth and then close it again, as if changing her mind about what she wanted to say. Or perhaps knowing that he couldn't be convinced. Because he couldn't be. "What this town needs is progress, not another inn like the one just down the street. Progress is the only way to move forward."

"To move forward? Or to move away from everything this town represents?" She stood up, barely looking him in the eye. "I should probably go. I still have work to do. Shopping and lists and planning for tomorrow."

"This isn't personal, Amelia," he said, even though it was, he knew. To him. "I'm just doing what I think is the best."

She turned to look at him when she reached the bottom of the porch steps. "Best for you? Or best for this town?"

"For...for both." He couldn't deny it. This opportunity wouldn't come along again and he didn't intend to blow it, and he certainly wasn't going to be foolish enough to let sentimentality stand in the way. His parents hadn't been willing to move with the times, to listen to the demands of the people, to adapt. He wouldn't make the same mistake. He'd promised himself that a long time ago.

She shook her head, backing away. "I should go. Thank you. For breakfast."

He nodded, unable to say anything more, and knowing that really it should be him thanking her, for bringing him back to this house, for opening a part of his memory that he'd blocked out over the years. But he couldn't bring himself to say it, not

when he wasn't so sure that coming here had helped at all.

Or if coming back to Blue Harbor was such a good idea after all.

7

Amelia arrived at the café earlier than usual the next day, hoping to push away some of the disappointment in her chest with a whisk and a bowl.

She tied her apron strings, noticing that her manicure was already started to chip. She shook her head, annoyed with herself for feeding into something so frivolous, and all because Matt Bradford was back in town? She should have known better. The man had resurfaced after a dozen years when he could have made the effort to come back years ago—and didn't. Really, the answer was as clear back then as it should be now.

With a sigh, she took two dozen eggs from the fridge and began cracking them into a large ceramic bowl, muttering to herself as she did so until she finally resorted to flicking on the radio to silence the noise in her head.

Even though she'd come back to the café yesterday afternoon, scoured the kitchen, made up her lists, and placed her orders for the week, and then went home to do all that laundry she had set aside on Sunday, she still couldn't shake the image of Matt's fancy new resort, or the horrible feeling that he was going to ruin this town for good. She could already picture the large, monstrous thing, so out of place in the rest of the community, glaring at everyone from the bay. Sure, it might draw more tourists to town, but she doubted any of them would want to trek down to her café for breakfast or lunch when they had more upscale accommodations at their fingertips.

Besides, she'd much rather keep the business she had if it meant keeping Blue Harbor as it was.

She was still muttering to herself when she took the big knife from the block and went to work on a pile of bell peppers, admittedly with more vigor than usual, and she hadn't even heard Maddie come in through the door until her sister started laughing.

"What's this I hear you grumbling about? Something about coming back and ruining the whole town?" Maddie slipped her apron from its hook and looped it over her neck. She gave Amelia a pitying look. "Is it safe to assume that your date didn't go well?"

Amelia set down her knife. "It wasn't a date," she corrected, even though she wasn't exactly sure what it had been at all. Maybe it could have been a date—if things hadn't gotten so derailed. It had sort of started off in that direction, with the bagels and the conversation. Truth be told, she'd originally wanted it to be a date. Hoped it would be. Even primped for it, in case it was.

She shook her head. What a fool. She of all people should have known that life didn't work that way. It wasn't some story in a book. Real life meant waking up, working hard, and running this café. It didn't mean that your old boyfriend would return to town years after abandoning it, claiming he'd been thinking of you every day since he'd left.

If that were the case, he wouldn't have stayed away so long in the first place!

Amelia gritted her teeth and went back to her chopping.

Maddie tied her apron strings behind her back and sighed. "I assumed so when you didn't come knocking on my door to tell me everything. That was part of our agreement, if you recall."

"I haven't forgotten," Amelia said. She minced a red pepper and moved on to a bright yellow one, which she sliced into long thing strips. "And I washed and ironed your dress last night. I'll return it tonight."

"No rush." Maddie gave her a little pat on the arm as she moved toward her station near the flour and sugar canisters and quickly went to work on her morning cinnamon rolls.

"And I'll be happy to give you the details. Well, not exactly happy." Amelia set down her knife and huffed. She didn't even know where to begin. With the disappointment over Matt's plans or the horrible realization that he had changed for the worse? Because the Matt she remembered would never have come up with such a design, especially not for Blue Harbor.

She decided to focus on the facts, not feed further into her own emotions. Eventually they would pass. Hopefully.

"Matt designed a resort that he's hoping will get built here in town," she said.

"A resort?" Maddie looked at her with interest. "That would be a first. Is there even land for that? It's pretty built up already. I think the only new addition we've seen in our lifetime is the yacht club!"

"I didn't even get into that," Amelia said. She added the sliced peppers to the arugula salad and her minced peppers to the beaten eggs. "I was too focused on how...how ugly the building was."

There. She had said it. The thing was ugly. Cold. Uninviting. Everything that Blue Harbor was not and should never be.

Maddie laughed. "Ugly? But you always used to praise his drawings when we were kids. I remember!"

As did Amelia. She had been his biggest fan back then. They'd seen the town through the same lens, and loved every inch of it. Together.

"Well, it would seem his tastes have changed since he's been gone!" Amelia put her quiche into the oven and set the timer. She grabbed a rag and wiped her hands, squaring her sister with a look. Maybe, it was more that he had changed. And that he didn't remember Blue Harbor or everything he once loved about it. That he didn't value all the things that he used to say made it special.

"It's a cement block, Maddie," she said, wincing at the mere memory of it.

"That doesn't sound right," Maddie said, her brow knitting in confusion. "How could he even think it would make sense?"

"He thinks this will be good for the local economy. That it will bring in more tourists, and year-round. He thinks that this is what people want. He thinks it's fresh."

Maddie's expression mirrored Amelia's thoughts so perfectly that no words needed to be exchanged.

Fresh! Amelia knew what was fresh, and that was the food she served here in the café, made with locally sourced ingredients, farm to table. She took pride in supporting the community. What Matt called "fresh" did not support the people of Blue Harbor, despite what he might think.

He'd been away too long, Amelia thought sadly. He'd forgotten the way this town functioned, and felt. He'd forgotten the heart of it.

Probably forgotten her too, if she was going to be honest with herself.

While she... She swallowed back that thought. No sense in dwelling on what couldn't be changed.

"Anyway," she said tersely. "I don't see any reason to continue to talk about Matt. What's done is done. We dated. We broke up. End of story."

Only it wasn't the end of the story, and Maddie knew it.

Her sister turned to her as her expression softened. "You loved him once."

"Once." Amelia nodded crisply. She struggled to keep the pull out of her chest when she remembered those years spent with Matt, and how he could make her laugh, and how he was always such easy company. She'd relied on him. Counted on him. Trusted him.

And...she'd missed him. Only the boy she'd missed no longer existed. Somewhere along the way he'd grown into a man whom she didn't recognize, at least not completely.

"Matt will be gone before long. With any luck this resort will never get built. And soon enough life will go back to normal."

Meaning boring, routine, and...a little bleak. She just hadn't thought of it that way up until Matt had returned and made her realize what she'd been missing.

Love. Excitement. A little pull in her chest that made her heart speed up with anticipation and hope. She'd dared to wish for things she never allowed herself to think about most days. Usually she worked until she was too tired to think about those things.

A fantasy, she reminded herself. The past. And if there was one thing that Matt did not want to hold onto or preserve, it was the past. He'd made that very clear.

"Is that really what you want?" Maddie didn't look any more convinced than Amelia felt. "To go back to the usual routine, with nothing to look forward to?"

"It's the way it has to be," Amelia said. She grinned at her sister, but it felt forced. "Besides, I happen to look forward to plenty around here. Time with my sisters, for example."

Maddie rolled her eyes. "You know what I mean."

Amelia did, of course, but she wasn't going to let herself be dragged down by it. With that, she walked over to bulletin board to look at her daily menu, her eyes drifting over to the contest that Maddie had tacked up last week. The deadline was certainly soon, and she doubted that she could devote the time to coming up with an entry as well as handle everything here at the café this week. But she couldn't resist the thought of putting the Firefly Café—and Blue Harbor—on the map.

And maybe showing a certain someone that a little old-fashioned café like hers could pull in business. And that this was exactly the kind of establishment that drew people to town, year after year, and season after season.

"Hey, Maddie?"

Maddie looked up from her butter and brown sugar mixture that was already filling the kitchen with a heavenly aroma.

"You think there's really time to enter this contest?"

Maddie grinned. "I think there's time. But you're not just going to enter. You're going to win."

Win. Imagine that!

Amelia unpinned the sheet from the board and set it down on the center island, as a reminder for the day.

And a reminder for why she was certain that Matt was going to make a big mistake. And that she may just have another way to prove that to him after all.

Before it was too late.

\*

Matt dropped down onto a bench on the docks that lent a panoramic view of the lakefront, from the harbor to the back of Main Street to the wide stretch of beach and the dense forest that curved around until it reached the neighboring town.

He'd tapped that particular spot as the best location for his resort, and not just because the acreage allowed for it. The green foliage would turn to shades of crimson and orange in the autumn, and be frocked with snow in the winter. All year round, the guests would be surrounded by trees on one side, and the lake on the other. They'd have a view of Evening Island, and be walking distance to the ferry port. They could walk or bike to town, and have the seclusion from it, too. He knew that the development team would go for it. He just had to be sure that the town would approve the plans, though he doubted they would have much room for argument with the pitch he had prepared.

He'd speak to the mayor, this week, and get it on the books for a vote before he went back to Minneapolis and cemented his plan.

He had already asked the research team to gather everything they knew about the targeted parcel of land, but that was the spot. He could see it. And he was already proud of it. Imagine! One of his buildings. A building all of his own. Right here in the town where his happiest memories had been formed.

And most of those memories were with Amelia.

He frowned when he thought of how they'd left things off yesterday. She didn't understand, but then, how could she? She'd never left town; it was all she knew. He could tell from the way that she and Britt were talking that it wasn't much easier for her than it had been for his parents, or half the other establishments in town. None of these businesses were thriving; they were just getting by. And some might not even be able to hold out. He'd seen the empty storefront beside Amelia's café.

She'd come around eventually, he told himself. When she saw the impact it had on her business, she'd be thanking him. Besides, her opinion was just one, and the opinions that mattered were that of the town council and his development team.

He had until next Friday to meet with the town council. The following Monday, he'd be back in the office. And then...

He pulled in a breath. Then everything would be right. Better than that, it would be as it should have been, all along.

It was early when he'd left Jackson's house, leaving his cousin to sleep away the morning after another late night tending bar, and he'd walked to town, despite the distance, lingering near the lakefront, taking photos for his presentation. Now, the morning was getting on. He checked his watch and decided it was late enough to put a call into the office, to see if the research team had any more feedback before he met with the mayor on Thursday.

"Bob!" He grinned in expectation when the analyst came on the line. "Tell me you have good news about the Blue Harbor resort project."

"That depends what you mean by good," Bob replied. Through the line, Matt could hear him take a sip of his coffee. A stalling tactic, no doubt.

Matt stifled a groan. He'd put so much thought and care into the design, creating not just a vision but a plan with enough to pull in tourists, and keep them coming back. It had to be different from what was already offered here in town, and it had to be bigger. Better.

It had to be rock solid.

Only now it would seem that there were a few cracks...

"That land you want? That's owned by the town."

Matt blinked out at the water. "I knew that already," he said, leaning back in relief.

It could happen. It would happen. It was all within reach.

"Well, you should know that we've discovered that there have been other permit applications for the space. Other people interested in it over the years."

Matt frowned again. "Developers?"

There was a shuffling of papers. "Some residential applications, and some business applications, too. Most appear to be related to fishing. I see one for a restaurant."

In other words, small offers. Nothing like the pitch that Matt had planned.

"Good information. Let me know if you find out anything more."

"Will do," said Bob. "Because the development team needs this buttoned up. They've been very selective about projects ever since they failed to find enough tenants to fill that office building in Chicago last spring."

"This is different," Matt said firmly. "Trust me, Bob. This resort is a slam dunk. It's exactly what the company needs."

And it was what this town needed. They just didn't know it yet.

8

At nine o'clock that night, Amelia snuffed out the last candle on the porch and walked into the empty dining room, her heart heavy when she turned the sign on the door.

"Another successful day," Rachel said from the behind the counter. It was her second summer working at the café, but Amelia knew it would likely be her last. She'd be starting her senior year of college in a few weeks. Amelia would have to find someone to fill her place for next year. It was all part of the process, but she'd still be sad to see Rachel go.

"Yep." Amelia knew she should agree with Rachel—after all, she hadn't had time to sit from the moment the café opened, and they'd even filled every table during the otherwise slow midafternoon hours—but she couldn't stop thinking about the fact that Matt hadn't stopped by to smooth things over from yesterday, and that maybe he didn't intend to.

Still, she didn't regret her words yesterday. It needed to be said. And if Matt was hell-bent on destroying the town he claimed to love so much, then she wasn't going to sit back quietly and watch.

She gave Rachel a tired smile. "Go ahead. I'll clean up."

Rachel hesitated, but briefly. "If you're sure."

"It's fine," Amelia said. She knew that Rachel had started dating Chip, one of the other seasonal staff who was helping Jackson over at the inn. She'd seen them getting ice cream last Sunday afternoon on her way back from the grocery store, and they had been sharing a sundae. One cherry on top. Two spoons. Chip had let her take it.

Actually, he'd spoon-fed it to her.

Amelia sighed. Even her father was spoon-fed by Candy—everything from chocolate-chip ice cream to greasy strips of bacon. Sure, this wasn't Amelia's idea of romance (unless, maybe, it involved a chocolate soufflé), but it served as another reminder that others had found love.

And she...had lost it.

"Oh good," Rachel said, as she quickly untied her apron. "Chip cuts out early tonight and we thought we'd check out that new band playing over at the pier."

"Sounds fun," Amelia said. The pier near the yacht club was a hot spot during the summer months—a gathering spot for live music and the occasional art show.

"You can join us?" Rachel smiled at her, but Amelia just shook her head. Maddie had already left, and Britt would be busy with Robbie and Keira, and Cora was probably still at her shop, poring over Christmas catalogues and ordering even more items for her already packed store. Gabby would probably be up for it. Maybe Gabby's younger sister, Jenna, too.

But Amelia just wanted to go home tonight. Her favorite reality show aired on Tuesday nights. Not that she'd be sharing that. It would just prompt more urging for her to get out of the house and socialize.

She waved goodnight to Rachel. Amelia sighed to herself as she wiped down all the tables and the flicked off the lights. That had never been her, had it? When she was in her early twenties, she was still living at home, still shuffling her college classes with helping out at the family orchard and making sure that her father was taken care of and her younger sisters were on the right path. Cora had gone to a local college as well, focused on business classes, because she'd always had her sights set on opening a holiday shop, and at her urging, Maddie followed suit, even if she would have been content to work at the orchard at the time.

It was cool outside when Amelia began her walk home, and the moon was full and bright, lighting up the sky and casting shadows along the lake water.

"You sure you should be walking alone at night?" a deep voice cut through the darkness.

Despite her usual comfort with exactly that, she jumped, and set a hand to her pounding heart. She stared in surprise—and admittedly, pleasure—at Matt, who was just a few yards away.

"Believe it or not, walking along the waterfront at night is one of the simple pleasures of this town," she remarked, still feeling a little defensive of the charm she held so dear. She jutted her chin. "You headed over to the pub?"

He shook his head. "Thought I'd check out that band that's playing tonight. Jackson mentioned it earlier."

Amelia nodded, suddenly wondering how different the night might have been if she had taken up Rachel's offer after all. She might have casually bumped into him, shared a drink, smoothed over the awkwardness between them. Now, it would be strange to turn around, claim she was going his same direction when she wasn't.

They were on different paths. Why couldn't she just accept that?

She managed a smile. "I see. Have fun."

Matt gave her a boyish grin, one eyebrow lifted in that way she could never resist. "You could join me? Jackson's working, and Robbie's home with

Keira and...Well, I didn't like the way we left things off yesterday," he said.

Amelia felt her shoulders slump as all her defenses sank. She wanted to stay mad at him, or at least disappointed in him, but when he talked to her like that, and smiled like that, and looked like that...Well, he made it pretty darn difficult.

"Me either," she said, waiting for him to close the distance between them with a few long strides. "I didn't mean to insult your design. I just—" She just wanted to make him see that it had no business in Blue Harbor. This town was quaint and yes, a little old fashioned, but that was what made it so appealing for so many.

But tonight wasn't the time for that. Tonight the only boy she had ever loved was standing beside her under the glow of the moonlight. It was summertime. The water was lapping quietly at the rocky shoreline.

And her television show could really wait.

And maybe, by being reminded of what made Blue Harbor so special, Matt would come to his senses all on his own.

"Look," Matt said. "The project hasn't even been approved. It might not even happen. But while I'm here, I'd like to make the most of it. What do you say? Let me buy you a glass of wine? The band can't be as bad at the Brad Fours."

Amelia burst out laughing, only now recalling the garage band that the four Bradford cousins had pulled together one summer, despite only Jackson being somewhat adequate on the guitar. It was short-lived once they realized they had no real talent, but now, thanks to the reminder, unforgettable.

"You make it really impossible to say no to you," she scolded, but she was grinning as they fell into step in the direction opposite her house and back toward town. As they rounded the shoreline, she could already hear the sounds of the music filling the night air, and see the strings of lights that had been set up from the dock posts, illuminating the dark sky.

A stand was set up for drinks, and Amelia was instantly surprised to see that Conway Orchard was sponsoring tonight's event.

"Britt?" She caught her sister's attention as they approached. "You didn't mention this to me."

"What can I say?" Britt didn't stop pouring drinks and collecting money as she talked. "I'm full of surprises."

She grinned at Amelia, for the first time noticing Matt beside her.

Britt's eyes narrowed just enough for Amelia to catch their true meaning. "And, it would seem, so are you."

"Robbie here tonight?" Matt asked, either not picking up on Britt's innuendo or deciding to ignore it.

Britt shook her head. "He's home with Keira. Not exactly the place for little kids. What can I get you guys?"

Matt turned to Amelia. "It's your family's company. What do you recommend?"

"Well, in that case, I suppose we should have my namesake," Amelia laughed. It was no surprise that the wine that had been named after her was a rosé (intended to match her hair color), and knowing now that Matt was more of beer drinker, she said, "But you might want to try the cider instead."

"Dad's favorite!" Britt handed them two glasses and refused to take Matt's money, saying he could get her back by featuring Conway's wines at his new, five-star resort.

"Robbie tells me that you're meeting with the mayor on Thursday," Britt added. "Good luck!"

Matt's smile was a little tight. "Thanks," was all he said.

Amelia averted her gaze, focusing instead on taking a long sip from her glass. If only Britt knew. And what would Britt say? She had a lot of experience with corporate restructuring from her previous job as a management consultant. She knew how to make a business a success. Would she think that this...this cinder block would be an asset to their small community? That a modern edge would really benefit any of them?

As the line for drinks grew, Amelia stepped aside to let Britt tend to everyone. She held her glass tightly as she and Matt moved through the crowd, finally finding a large rock to sit on, a little closer than she might have planned—not that she was complaining.

"My sister is full of big business ideas, in case you haven't noticed," she remarked. "She had a big job in Chicago before she moved back. She's hell-bent on making the family business a thriving success."

"Good for her," Matt said.

"I think she worries too much, if you ask me," Amelia said mildly. "The business has been around for generations."

"You can never get too comfortable," Matt replied.

Amelia decided to let that little comment slip, instead choosing to focus on the unexpected turn of events. The clear sky. The wonderful music. The warmth of Matt's body beside hers; a sharp contrast to the cool breeze coming in off the lake.

"I'm pretty comfortable," she admitted, and not just because she was sitting beside him on this beautiful night. The band wasn't half-bad either. "I love running my café."

Matt nodded thoughtfully. "It's important to do what you love."

She'd never thought of that before, but she supposed it was true. "I guess I took it for granted. We grew up in a family business, and we all went on to pursue what we were passionate about, too. I suppose we were fortunate."

"Very fortunate," he said, giving her a long look.

Now she'd done it. Stuck her foot in her mouth. Drawn attention to the dark cloud that hung over them; the reason that he had left town in the first place.

"Can I ask you a question?" When he looked at her like that, with his eyes so earnest, so intense in their hold on hers, she wondered if she even had the nerve. It would be easier to drop the past, just like he seemed to want to do. But the past was a part of her. It had made her who she was today.

"Why didn't you ever write? Or call?"

He closed his eyes briefly, and then took a sip of his cider. "I meant to, Amelia. I wanted to."

"We never officially ended things," she said. "Not really. I mean, you were moving away, and...it was all up in the air. I thought you'd be back to visit. I thought it would just be different. Not over."

Matt nodded. "I was young. We both were. But—I thought of you, Amelia. Every day. For a long time. I thought of everyone in this town."

She tipped her chin, giving him a long look. "Please. If you missed us all that much you would have come back, stayed with your cousins. Called. Something."

Matt was quiet as he sipped his drink. "I wasn't a part of this world anymore. I was starting over, in a new town. I guess...it was just easier to focus on my new life, not the one I had lost."

"You didn't have to lose it, though," she said.

He looked at her, his jaw tensing. "Yes, Amelia, I did. My dad lost his business and then the house. My life was somewhere else."

She decided to let it drop, knowing that there was truth in what he was saying. He had to adjust to his new life. She understood that much, on a different level. When her mom was gone, in many ways, it was like starting over. They'd all been forced to adjust to a new way of life, and sometimes, holding onto the old ways only reminded her of what she no longer had.

They listened to the next song in silence, and every once in a while she could feel his eyes on hers. A few times she even looked his way, catching his stare, offering him a slow smile.

"I'm glad we did this," Matt said, when the band took a break.

Amelia had enjoyed herself more than she had for a Tuesday night in longer than she could remember, and she was sad to think of the night ending, even though she was pretty sure that ending it was the best thing that she could do right now. It would be easy to fall for him again, to go back to that part of her life that was so happy, and full, and think that they could carry on where they had left off.

But chances were that Matt would be leaving town soon.

If he didn't destroy it first.

"I should probably call it a night. Restaurant hours and all." Meaning that she would be out of the house before five.

She stood, her foot slipping as she stepped off the rock, and she reached for Matt's shoulder, squaring herself. His gaze was intense when she caught his eye, and she was happy that he couldn't see her cheeks flush in the moonlight, because oh, she could feel them burn.

Without a word, he took her hand, helping her down slowly. His palm was smooth, warm, and so familiar that she could have held it all night. Instead, she dropped it quickly, feeling flustered and a little unsure of her footing, even though she was now on solid ground.

His gaze dropped down to her mouth, and for a moment, she wondered if he might kiss her.

Her heart sped up. No good would come from that.

She turned, so they were no longer face to face, so she wouldn't be tempted to want something that she couldn't have.

"You sure you're safe getting home?"

She just grinned at him. She would have liked the company on the walk home, but she also knew that Jackson lived in the opposite direction. And she wasn't exactly sure what would happen if she did let Matt come to her apartment. There was still something between them—a connection that she couldn't deny. A comfort and familiarity that made it a little more difficult to resist his charms than she probably should.

After all, Matt was an outsider now, more so than the tourists who paid homage every year. He didn't appreciate this lovely little town for what it was and what it had always been. He wanted to change it.

And she wanted it to remain just as it always had been.

In every possible way, she thought, as she gave him one last wave goodnight.

*

Matt turned and left Amelia. It was late, but not terribly late, and he was restless. Spending time with her calmed him, made him forget about all his troubles or anxiety or even the past. But once she was gone, it all stirred to the surface again, along with new thoughts...ones that were exclusively about her, and what was happening between the two of them.

He decided to stop by Robbie's house on the way back to Jackson's, even if it was a bit out of the way. The lights to the cottage were on when he pulled into the driveway and turned off his engine, but just in case, he knocked on the door instead of ringing the bell, so he didn't wake Keira.

Robbie answered the door quickly, looking pleased to find him standing there. "You want to come in for a drink?"

Matt wasn't sure what he had expected to find at Robbie's house. A bachelor pad similar to his own, he supposed, or even something like Jackson's apartment. Something sparse and functional. Instead what he walked into was a home, with framed photos hanging on the walls and lining the mantle. The refrigerator was covered in paintings and drawings that Keira had made, and there was even a bowl of fruit on the center of the counter.

Robbie caught him gaping at it and laughed. "It's the only way I remember to tell Keira to eat a piece of fruit each day. If it were up to her, she'd live on pizza."

"Is there anything wrong with that?" Matt grinned and accepted the bottle of beer.

"Nothing wrong with it if it was just me, and we did eat our fair share of pepperoni and cheese after Stephanie..." He trailed off, lowering his eyes.

"I'm sorry," Matt said. He knew from Jackson that Robbie had taken the death of his wife badly. It was the reason he had returned to Blue Harbor, after leaving not long before Matt had. But he wasn't just sorry that Robbie had lost his wife. He was also sorry that he'd never met her. He hadn't attended the wedding. Neither had his brother or parents.

Robbie pulled himself together and forced a grin. "We've learned to keep forward. Being back in town helps. Boston was great, but there's no place like home."

Home. Matt took a long sip of his beer. He wasn't so sure where home was anymore, or if he really even had one.

"I was down at the dock tonight and ran into Britt," Matt told him as they made their way out onto the back deck. He noticed that Robbie didn't slide the door closed all the way. No doubt he was keeping an ear out for Keira.

He marveled at this as he settled into a chair. His cousin had grown up while he'd been away. He'd gone through hell and back, and come out stronger. Matt wasn't so sure he could say the same for himself.

"Ah yes." Robbie grinned at the mention of Britt. It was clear that even after all these years, she sparked something in him that he hadn't found with anyone else. "She's full of big ideas. Did it seem like people were buying drinks?"

"Oh yeah," Matt assured him.

"You went with Jackson?" Robbie asked.

Matt stalled by sipping his drink, knowing that he had to come clean before Britt told him the next day. Which she would. He knew how those Conway girls were. "I ran into Amelia, so we went together."

A knowing smile tipped Robbie's mouth, and even in the moonlight, Matt could see the gleam in his eye.

"Stop," he warned. "You sound like Jackson."

Robbie held up his hands. "Did I say anything?"

"You didn't have to," he said.

"I'm just going to say," Robbie said, leaning forward. "That this isn't such a bad town. And maybe, like me, you'd be happy if you came back."

Maybe, but then their reasons for leaving and returning were entirely different, like everything else in their lives.

"The Conway girls are pretty special," Robbie continued.

Matt gave him the side eye. Still, it was the truth. "You don't need to tell me that. Amelia's great, but—"

141

"No but," Robbie said. "She's great. No sense trying to deny it."

No, there really wasn't.

They finished their beers, talking about business, reminiscing on the old days, like the time that they'd lost their oars to Robbie's parents' canoe and had to swim all the way back to shore. Matt was laughing by the time the evening had wound down, and he was disappointed to leave.

He realized with a start that he'd feel the same way when it came time to go back to Minneapolis.

"Thanks for letting me drop by," he said, making his way to the door.

"You kidding me? Thanks for stopping by." Robbie laughed. "Before Britt and I got back together, the evenings were the longest part of the day. Keira in bed and the house to myself. Only the television for company. That gets old."

Yes, Matt thought. It did.

"Guess you could say that I've gotten used to having Britt around. With her out tonight, I was feeling a little restless."

"I can understand that," Matt said, giving his cousin a thump on the shoulder.

"Those Conway girls," Robbie said, shaking his head.

Matt just grinned as he let himself out. He could understand that, too. And for as different as their lives had gone in recent years, in many ways, he and Robbie were more alike than he'd thought. They'd both left town. They'd both returned. And they both still had a Conway girl on their minds.

9

Amelia spent the next two days experimenting with her contest entry every chance that she had, and by Thursday afternoon, she had finally narrowed things down to three options.

She called over to Maddie, who was staying late to help with the early weekend crowd, and handed her a fork.

"Be honest," she said, and Maddie just shot her a look that told Amelia she needn't worry about that. It was true, that as sisters, they'd each fallen into certain roles, even if things did shake up a bit when their mother died. Maddie was always direct—when asked—but she was also very private when it came to her own life and her own feelings. As hard of a time as Maddie may have given her about not getting out and dating more, Amelia could easily say the same for Maddie. And Cora.

Maddie tried each dish without commenting. She chewed slowly, as if trying to memorize the flavors, and then set her fork into the sink before turning to Amelia.

"I'm thinking you go with the pasta," she said.

Amelia grimaced, not because she didn't think the pasta stood a fair chance, but because she was leaning more toward the flatbread, which was so colorful with the sprinkle of arugula on top.

"What about the whitefish?" She felt compelled to have a fish entry, considering they were a lake-front town.

"I'd go with the pasta," Maddie said. "Everyone loves pasta."

Amelia wasn't going to argue with that point, but still, she decided to add all three options to her list of dinner specials and see how her customers responded. The entry was due by tomorrow, and the winners would be announced next week. It wasn't a big competition, but it was state-wide, and like Maddie had said, it was an opportunity to put their business on the map.

She went into the dining room with her chalk pen and wrote out the specials on the board, just as she did every day. Usually the specials focused on a seasonal flavor, often she used some fruits from her family's orchard, but tonight she was on a mission. She was collecting information.

And she wasn't the only one.

Thanks to Britt, she now knew that Matt was meeting with the mayor today to discuss his plans for the new project. She didn't know what she was holding her breath for more, really: that Matt's project would meet resistance or that it would succeed and keep him here.

If only he would come to his senses!

A tap on her shoulder made her jump and she turned, heart thumping with the hope of seeing Matt, to see Candy grinning back at her.

"Maybe one day you can put my famous cheese biscuits on that specials board." She winked, dramatically, and despite her reservations, Amelia couldn't help but smile.

Candy was a passionate woman, and if her biscuits were as good as she claimed them to be, then maybe she should cut her a break. But not today. Today she needed to focus on her contest entry, and hopefully use it to get her mind off of Matt Bradford.

"Next time I'm over at the house I'll try one," she promised. Candy hadn't officially moved into the house on Water Street yet, but it was nearly a sure bet that if Amelia dropped by, Candy would be there.

"Perfect! I'm making a whole platter of them Sunday." Candy rubbed her hands together eagerly.

Amelia blinked at Candy, distracted. "Sunday?" While they used to gather for Sunday dinners on a regular basis, they'd fallen away from that established routine recently.

Candy's eyes flew open. "This Sunday night! It's Britt's birthday dinner!"

Of course. She hadn't forgotten. Except that she had, and not just because Britt's birthday wasn't technically until September. She'd been so distracted with thoughts of Matt and the project and the conflicting emotions that tumbled in waves that she had sheer forgotten that she should buy a gift, and probably contribute at least a side-dish, too.

"I forgot we were celebrating early," she said.

Candy shrugged. "Only time everyone was free!"

"What can I bring?" she asked, thinking of her best crowd-pleasers. Pasta salad, perhaps, the one with the pistachios and feta? Or maybe her cornbread. But then, that would probably compete with Candy's biscuits.

"What? Or who?" Candy gave a wicked grin.

Amelia shifted the weight on her feet, not amused.

"Just your pretty self!" Candy said with a dismissive wave. "I know how busy all you girls are, so you just leave it all to me!"

Normally this sort of statement on Candy's part might have felt like overstepping, but today, Amelia was grateful for it. For so many years, she had planned every holiday, cooked for every family dinner, felt responsible for making sure that everyone was provided for. And now, someone had come along to give her a hot meal, and a day off. Even if Candy did love nothing more than a stick of butter and a frying pan.

"Thanks, Candy," she said, meaning it. She tried to remember the details that Candy had sent out weeks earlier. "I'll be there at four. Are Gabby and Jenna able to make it, too?"

Her Uncle Steve's three girls had been just as close as sisters growing up, but now Brooke rarely visited, and Jenna worked evening and weekend hours as a piano teacher, so they didn't spend as much time together as they did when they were young.

"Gabby is bringing the centerpieces," Candy replied. "I'm thinking...pink! And white! Oh, it's going to be so pretty!" Candy clasped her hands together. Her eyes sparkled.

"Are you sure I can't bring something?" Amelia asked, feeling guilty.

"If you must bring something, you can bring a date!" Candy gave her a knowing look, and Amelia felt her cheeks grow hot. Candy really wasn't going to let this go, but then, why would Amelia ever think she might?

"But I'm not..." Oh boy. Now Candy's teeth were bared into a wide smile.

"You raised my suspicions when I saw you at the salon," Candy said. "After all, a girl doesn't go from having her sister trim her hair to suddenly getting all glammed up without good reason. So, I did a little digging about that strapping cousin of Robbie's..."

In other words, a little gossiping.

"And I heard that you and Matt Bradford used to be quite the item! And word is that he's back in town!"

"That was a long time ago, Candy," Amelia said wearily. "He just wanted to say hello. That's all." She turned to go back into the kitchen, but Candy followed her right in.

The look of horror on Maddie's face didn't go unnoticed—at least not by Amelia—but Maddie quickly composed herself and went back to prepping for the dinner service.

"What's this?" Candy held up the contest rules with interest, shifting away when Amelia tried to snatch it back.

She exchanged a look with Maddie, and sighed. "It's a contest, Candy. Best café in the state."

"And you're entering! Can I vote?"

Amelia opened her mouth with a comeback before realizing that none was needed. She swallowed the lump in her throat, humbled. That was one thing you had to say about Candy. She cared. A lot. And while it may have felt a bit intense at times, she really couldn't say that she'd prefer it another way.

Except when Candy was barging into her kitchen, that was.

"I think so?" She looked to Maddie for confirmation, who just nodded. "Yes, I guess that the entire town can vote!"

She had just assumed that based on her photos and description, she would collect the online votes she needed, but now, she realized that she needed the community's support.

Just like she needed Candy's.

"You've just given me an idea, Amelia!" Candy pressed her lips together firmly, but her eyes were positively dancing. "I am going to make it my mission to get every single person in town to vote for your café." She shook the contest sheet. "Can I keep this?"

All the information she needed was available online, anyway, so Amelia nodded. "Sure."

Maddie gave her a hooded look when Candy left a minute later, waving her sheet and muttering to herself about flyers.

"You have to admit, she likes to be helpful," Maddie remarked.

Amelia laughed under her breath, but a fresh wave of hope filled her again. If enough people voted, she just might win. And if she won, Matt—and the planning committee—might just be swayed to see what really brought people to this town year after year, and it wasn't a concrete block on the waterfront.

Who would have known? Maybe Candy was going to be the one to save this town after all.

After all, she'd already saved their family in many ways, even if it wasn't easy to admit.

*

Matt sat in the lobby of the Town Hall, an old building that blended in with the others: white with black shutters, and even window boxes filled with bright red geraniums. He tapped his foot anxiously against the worn floorboards and eyed the mayor's office door before checking his watch again. He'd arrived early, but then he'd been advised by the spectacled assistant that there would be a delay, so he'd been waiting for close to an hour, and that did little to help his nerves.

Finally, just when he'd been about to stand and stretch his legs, the door opened and his former neighbor Mr. Hudson—now technically Mayor Hudson—emerged.

"Sorry about the wait," he said with a tired smile.

Matt accepted his extended hand and shook it. "It's good to see you again." He'd always liked the Hudsons. They were friendly neighbors who took pride in their garden—Mrs. Hudson was forever tending to her roses, and giving a friendly wave when Matt emerged from the house. They'd had two golden retrievers that were Mr. Hudson's pride and joy, even if they seemed to loyally follow at his wife's feet as she roamed their manicured lawn, stopping every once and a while to pull a weed.

The mayor closed the door to his office and motioned for Matt to take a seat. "When I saw that I had a meeting with Matthew Bradford on my calendar, I have to say that I was intrigued. How long has it been?"

"More than twelve years," Matt replied, adjusting his tie.

The mayor, he saw, was dressed casually, in khakis and a seersucker shirt that was rolled at the sleeves, and Matt now wondered if he'd overdressed, looked like he was trying too hard, or if Amelia was right, if life in the city had changed him.

He frowned slightly, refusing to go down that path just now. He had a sketch in his portfolio, and a vision that he was excited about. Now to just get the mayor's approval, and he'd have all the support he needed when it came time to present his plan in a town meeting.

"How are your folks?" the mayor asked, and for a moment, Matt felt an old wound tear open.

His father had landed on his feet—eventually—and still worked at the same construction company he'd started at once they settled in Minneapolis. His mother kept busy in her vegetable garden and working part-time at the library. She was content, and by now, the small house they lived in was home for them. Or so they said. There was no mention of how holidays used to be, with all the festive energy that came from a big table and lively conversation, the excitement that Matt and his brother and cousins shared each Christmas Eve. Now their holidays were quiet, just the four of them, and even though it had been that way for a long time, it still felt wrong. Sometimes, when his mother set out the small turkey on Thanksgiving, he wondered if she remembered the holidays that they used to share, with so much food that they all had leftovers for a week. Or if his father remembered the Winter Carnival, and the tree-lighting in the town square.

He cleared his throat. "They're well, thanks."

Then, with all the confidence he could muster, he leaned forward and spread out his plans. "As you know, Blue Harbor has never had a full-service resort. It would be the first of its kind, and in addition to adding tax revenue to the town, I think it would be enough of an attraction to lure tourists year-round."

The mayor looked thoughtful as he studied the list of amenities planned for the project. "You certainly kept the winter climate in mind. The spa alone could draw tourists looking for a relaxing escape."

Matt pushed back his excitement and nodded. "And the lakefront location is key, as I'm sure you understand."

"It's certainly a more modern look than we're used to," the mayor said frankly.

Matt had prepared himself for this sort of push-back. "I think you'll find that it's part of the appeal. Similar properties in other well-known resort areas have had great success over the years." He slid a paper across the desk and waited while the mayor read it, his eyebrows rising at what he saw.

Matt decided to push the topic. "There are plenty of older buildings in town. Plenty of landmark status inns for tourists to fill. This wouldn't compete with existing business. It would draw new people to town. People who may not have considered Blue Harbor in the past."

The mayor seemed to mull this over as he peered closer at the papers.

"I know it's not traditional," Matt pressed, "but it's new. And it's a little different. Sure, there are stone walls instead of picket fences, and it's not made of wood, but it's fresh...and well, I think it could benefit the town."

"And you," the mayor said wryly, glancing up at him.

Matt held up his hands. "I'd like to think of it as a win-win. I care about this town, Mayor Hudson. My biggest regret was having to leave it. I'd like to think that this is an opportunity to help grow the town, not change it."

The mayor leaned back in his chair, tenting his fingers in thought. "There's a town council meeting next Friday. We'll put it to a vote then. In the meantime, can I get copies of these?"

Matt nodded eagerly. "Those are yours to keep. And I look forward to the meeting. Thank you, Mayor. For...the opportunity."

"There is one thing I'd like to ask you to consider," the mayor said, deflating Matt's spirits. "The location has never been an easy sell, and several have tried. We like our green space, and that particular spot is slated to become designated park land. Would you be willing to consider an alternate location?"

Matt hadn't known there would be another option, and racked his brain to think of where along the shoreline he could find enough space.

"There's a spot behind Main Street, in between the harbor and the beach," the mayor was saying.

Matt nodded along, trying to pull up a visual image of the location the mayor was referring to. His mouth went dry.

"You mean, where the Firefly Café is located?"

The mayor nodded. "Strange location for a café, if you ask me. Would be better suited for Main Street, really. The businesses back there are off the path, unnoticed by many tourists, and the tenant that shares the building with Amelia Conway closed nearly a year ago. One of those over-priced paper shops," he added, dismissing the notion with a wave of his hand. "We have a couple of other boutiques back there, and I've been encouraging their owners to relocate to Main Street for years now, especially with a couple of the storefronts on that stretch vacant. I just haven't had a convincing argument until now."

Until now. Meaning until Matt came back to town and presented the mayor with a better idea. And one that would put Amelia out of her café for good.

"I do think the clientele we're targeting for this sort of resort would prefer something more secluded, away from the traffic of Main Street," Matt said honestly. Still, the appeal of being so close to shops and restaurants could appeal to them, as well. He could picture the rear lined with tall arbor vitae, creating a natural fence around the great building.

"I understand, but that might not be an option," Mayor Hudson continued. He looked at Matt frankly. "It wouldn't take much to sway most of those businesses to relocate. And for anyone who puts up resistance, well, this might be a case of eminent domain. Like you said, a project like this could really boost our local economy."

Meaning they could force Amelia to sell if she didn't go quietly. Matt felt his mouth go dry.

"We'll see what the council says." The mayor stood, signaling the end of the meeting.

Matt shook the man's hand and walked out the door, his heart pounding as he pushed down the long hallway and out into the late afternoon sunshine. Main Street was bustling, with tourists and locals, and Matt wondered if maybe the mayor was right. If shops that were off the beaten path, without the same exposure and signage, would benefit from a new location. Maybe, it was just what Amelia needed to bolster her through the lean winter months.

He decided to drop by her café. Just to feel that theory out.

*

Amelia passed another order to Rachel, who raised her eyebrows. "Looks like we have a clear favorite for your contest entry," she remarked.

It was still early into dinner service, but it was true that the flatbread was wildly popular; enough so that Amelia made a mental note to include it on the menu again tomorrow, if not permanently.

"It's a full house," Sonia remarked, coming through the kitchen door with a flushed face that meant she was overworked, or had spent too much time out on the patio when the sun was still strong.

Rachel had the kitchen covered for now, and Amelia said to Sonia, "Take a ten-minute break. I'll take over the patio."

"Maddie's got the front room covered," Sonia said. Her smile was grateful. It was her first season at the café and Amelia hoped that it wouldn't be her last. "Thanks."

Amelia was happy to be out of the hot kitchen. Sure, she loved to cook, but she also loved interacting with her customers, tending to the counter, and of course, watching everyone enjoy their experience—and their food. There were the occasional complaints, but it was all part of running a business, and she'd learned over time to settle things, take the heat, and move on. The customer was always right, as the saying went.

Except when the customer was Matt Bradford.

She stopped in her tracks when she stepped out onto the patio. She felt her cheeks flush and she had the overwhelming urge to turn, walk around, back inside, and not leave the kitchen for the rest of the night, but then of course, that wouldn't exactly be professional. And she had sent Sonia off on a break. Damn it!

With a pounding heart, she put on a pleasant smile as she approached his table, where he was studying the menu with interest. He was at her place of business, after all. Meaning, he had sought her out.

Memories of their evening the other night made her breath catch. He'd almost kissed her. She was sure of it. And she'd almost let him.

She couldn't be sure she'd be able to resist next time.

She stiffened, remembering that he'd met with the mayor today. Was he coming to tell her news? She didn't even want to know. What would be the better outcome at this point?

"Good evening," she said, coming to stand beside his table.

It was a beautiful evening, with the boats bobbing in the water and the sound of the crickets just beginning to chirp. But was it a good evening? Time would tell.

He smiled up at her, as casually as if the other day had never happened, and she wondered if maybe she'd read too far into it; if things didn't need to be as awkward as they felt.

She waited to see if he would mention the meeting, but he said nothing, just looked up at her with that irresistible grin that made her stomach roll over.

She swallowed hard. Getting personal down at the docks had been one thing. But now she was at work. And she was on a mission.

And it really didn't matter that she could still recall the touch of his hand on hers, or the heat of his body, so close. What mattered was that he intended to either ruin her town or leave it. And neither option boded well for a potential romance.

"Have you been helped yet?" There, see, this wasn't so bad. She would keep things breezy, stay professional. She was on the clock, after all, even if she was the boss.

"What do you recommend?" he asked, leaning back and hooking his ankle over his knee, as if he intended to get comfortable and stay a while.

She chewed her lip, thinking that they weren't really getting anywhere by dancing around the topic like this, unless of course, there was nothing to discuss. They were just two people who used to date. Half a lifetime ago.

"We have a few specials tonight. The flatbread is very popular. It's topped with fresh arugula from my own garden. We also have a lovely tomato tart with goat cheese from Trotter's Farm. Everything on the menu is seasonal."

He nodded approvingly. "Interesting strategy."

She narrowed her eyes. "It's not a strategy. I like to keep things fresh. And I like to give business to the local farms, including my own family's orchard."

"That's a sensible approach. Businesses helping businesses." He hesitated for a moment. "Do you ever think you'd be better off with a location on Main Street?"

Her mouth slacked. But then, she supposed that she had given him a hard time about his work. Maybe he was just giving her a taste of how it felt to be on the defense.

"I'm only one block off from Main Street," she replied. "Besides! Who can beat this waterfront location?"

She attributed the patio to her biggest driver from spring through early fall, when she put heat lamps on the deck to keep people outdoors for a few weeks longer.

"Just wondering," he said, but he didn't meet her eye.

She could feel the question build up inside her, bursting to come out, needing to know. It was evening by now, meaning his meeting with the mayor had come and gone. And what had come of it?

She decided that it didn't matter. Matt Bradford was someone she had cared about an awful lot, once. But he was part of her past. And now, she had to focus on her future. And that meant getting through this shift and putting the finishing touches on her contest recipe.

Besides, she had a sneaking suspicion that Matt hadn't come here to gloat. From the weary look in his eyes, she had the unsettling impression that he had come to apologize.

She licked her lips before something could be said that would lead to another argument between them. "Can I bring you a beer?"

He nodded. "And I'll try that flatbread," he said. "You really sold me on it."

She could only hope he wasn't the only one.

"Amelia—"

She had just started to go back into the building, but now she turned to him, her heart pounding. "Yes?"

He stared at her for what felt like minutes, his expression one of clear regret. And she knew, the way she knew what her sisters meant when they said nothing, but simply met her eye, that the mayor had approved his design.

"Just...don't rush on my behalf. I can see you're busy, and I'm happy to sit here and take in the view. It really is a lovely view."

She nodded, and with a heavy heart went into the café and straight to the kitchen.

She passed the ticket to Sonia as soon as she returned from her break. "This is for the man at table four," she replied.

One perk of being the owner, she thought. She didn't have to face Matt again tonight if she didn't want to, and right now, she didn't think she could.

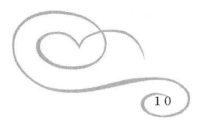

10

Amelia knew that she didn't have to bring any food to Britt's birthday party, but it didn't stop her. Maddie swung by the café after the market and together they made two dozen of the strawberries and cream cupcakes that their mother used to make for Britt each year on her birthday while Rachel and Sonia handled the dwindling lunch crowd. Maddie even remembered exactly how their mother decorated them—with pink sprinkles and a sliced strawberry in the center of the buttercream frosting, so everyone had a hint of what was inside.

"Perfectly fit for a ten-year-old girl," Amelia laughed, but it warmed her heart to look at them just the same. She could still picture Britt as a young girl, grinning broadly when their mother lit the candles on her cupcakes and they all broke into song.

These were the happy memories that she'd tried to cling to over the years, even when the images of more difficult times tried to push to the forefront. These were the reasons she had stayed. All these memories were a part of her. And of this town.

Maddie looked out the window of the café. "I could use some fresh air. Want to walk home?"

Home. Amelia still liked the sound of that, even though the house in town they shared was technically home now.

"Sure," she said. There would be plenty of chilly autumn nights and winter snowfalls to warrant the car, and like most people who lived in the region, when the warm weather finally came, they were careful to make the most of it—flinging open windows, eating outside, and stretching out the evening long past sunset. Normally, they might have biked it, but Amelia didn't want to risk putting the cupcake containers in her bicycle basket.

"It feels nice to keep Mom's recipes going," she said to Maddie as they packed up the cupcakes and headed out into the warm sunshine. It was the first time they'd be celebrating Britt's birthday together since she'd gone away to college and then settled in Chicago, and Amelia hoped that she would appreciate the gesture. There was a time when just the mention of their mother would bring Britt to tears, leave her distant and silent and cut off for weeks. Now that she was back in town, that had changed. Like the rest of them, she'd learned that it was better to keep the memories alive rather than banish them.

Amelia wondered if eventually Matt might feel the same. If he'd come to remember what he loved about this town before it was too late.

"It's why I make my pies each week," Maddie said. "I sold out this morning again."

"You sell out every Sunday morning at the market," Amelia teased.

Amelia had been waiting for an opportunity to ask Maddie about her long-term plans. She'd been helping out at the café for years, but Amelia had never expected her to stay forever. It was a good experience for Maddie, and Amelia appreciated the help, not to mention that she saw it as her responsibility to give Maddie a place to come to every day until she figured out exactly what it was she wanted to do with her life. She hated to see her sister leave the café, but at the same time, she knew that Maddie had grown up, that she was ready to do something on her own.

That she'd be okay. Just like their father. Just like Cora. And Britt.

And even her, Amelia thought. Sure, she may not have found love, but she had the café.

"How was the market today?" she asked, as they turned onto the street that led down to the waterfront. Their childhood house was at the far end, and even now, at the age of thirty, when she had her own apartment and business and furnishings, and life, this gabled Victorian that backed up to the lake was still home.

"Oh, you know how it's always busy this time of the year," Maddie said. "I feel bad. My pies were in such demand that I didn't save one for dinner tonight."

Amelia held up the cupcake tray. "We have these."

Maddie nodded. They were quickly approaching the house. Amelia felt another opportunity slipping away.

"Have you given any more thought to Britt's suggestions?" Amelia was aware that Britt had encouraged Maddie to do more with the pies, to sell them at the market in volume, and enlist the help of other staff to help. But she'd backed off when she realized that Maddie didn't share her enthusiasm, and Amelia couldn't say she blamed her. Their mother had made pies for the market each Sunday as a way of sharing her joy for baking with the members of town. And Maddie made the pies to carry on that tradition.

But Maddie was too talented to just help out around the café indefinitely. She had something to offer all on her own. Something, like their mother, to share.

"I don't like the idea of mass producing pies for the orchard. It's not about profit to me," she said firmly. "Some things are better off just as they are, you know?"

Amelia stopped walking and grinned at her sister. "Well said, Maddie."

Maddie gave her a little grin. "I learned from the best."

Amelia didn't know in that moment if Maddie meant their mother or her, but either way, she smiled against the tears that burned the back of her eyes and tipped her chin toward the house.

"Sunday night dinner."

"Just like old times," Maddie sighed.

If only, Amelia couldn't help but think.

*

This Sunday night dinner was proving to be nothing like old times, Amelia quickly saw. For starters, the dinner that Candy had prepared was not dinner at all, at least not in the traditional sense of the word.

Amelia stood in dining room, staring at the buffet that had been assembled on the formal cherry wood table that had once belonged to her grandmother, and that her mother used to enlist them to polish, once a week. The chairs had been moved to the front living room so there would be more seating for the guests. The plates that were in a stack were made of plastic. Pink plastic. To match the pink plastic cups and the giant balloons that revealed Britt's exact age. Seeing as she was only thirty-three, this probably wasn't a total travesty, but still, Amelia made a mental note to not let Candy plan anything once they all neared forty.

If Candy was still around by then. Though, by the way things were going, that was likely.

Amelia pulled in a sigh, trying to suppress the emotions that were building inside her. Whoever said there was no place like home hadn't met Candy. Yes, Amelia was in the very house where she had grown up, but the traditions that she and her sisters had worked to uphold were now replaced with Candy's vision. Gone were the days of gathering around this very table with a roast and sides, or a giant lasagna, fresh from the oven, with Cora and Maddie arguing who would get the corner slice of garlic bread.

Amelia wasn't even half sure what she was looking at, and she gingerly poked a ball of dough that sat in a basket with others, trying to determine if it was a sweet or a savory.

"Oh, goodie, you found my cheese biscuits!" Candy sang from where she stood in the entrance to the kitchen, her hair bigger and blonder than usual, her eyes shining. "Now don't be shy! Go on, fill those plates! I have more coming! After all, it's not every day I get to a host a party for one of Denny's girls."

Britt caught Amelia's eye across the room, saying nothing, yet speaking everything.

Candy was trying her best. She cared. She wanted to do something nice for them. Britt saw it, even appreciated it.

But in that moment, Amelia had never missed her mother more.

She pushed the ache away, reminding herself that it was Britt's day, and it was Britt who had perhaps handled their mother's loss the hardest. She was the oldest. She'd known her the longest. This wasn't easy for any of them, but she wasn't going to make it any more difficult than it needed to be.

She watched as her cousins Gabby and Jenna exchanged a glance and then, gingerly, loaded their plates. It was what it was, she supposed. Her new reality. May as well try to make the most of it.

With a large gulp she took a bite of the "famous" cheese biscuit and, as much as she hated to admit, found that it was rather delicious. Unhealthy, yes, but...surprising. And oddly similar to one of Candy's all-encompassing hugs. Soft. Warm. Even a little comforting.

She bypassed the multi-colored gelatin mold and the mini sausages wrapped in pastry, wishing she had brought a salad instead of the cupcakes. The tuna casserole was the only crowd pleaser, but the heavy hand of dark orange cheese made her pause, and she stepped away, deciding that she would opt instead for another...cheese biscuit.

"Told you you'd love 'em!" Candy's carefully shaped eyebrows wiggled as she came into the room, setting another tray on the table. Cora was quick to slide a pot holder under the tray before it went down, and Amelia could practically hear all four sisters breathe a collective sigh of relief.

Amelia considered the newest option. Corn dogs. Beside Robbie, Keira practically squealed in delight.

"It's just like a trip to the carnival, Daddy!" She smiled widely as she eagerly reached for a handful to add to her plate. Candy looked on with approval.

Amelia stuffed a cheese biscuit into her mouth to keep from laughing out loud, and turned to go into the living room—and straight into the chest of Matt Bradford.

They stood in the hallway, at the base of the stairs that was lined with all their baby and toddler portraits, and, of course, their parents' wedding photo.

She attempted to chew the cheese biscuit, but it was large, and soft, and...large. Very, very large.

Matt watched her with a strange sort of interest, waiting patiently for her to finish, rather than move aside, or let her dash away, or perhaps hand her a napkin, which she could have used to shield her face, which was now burning with embarrassment.

She attempted to move the biscuit to her cheek, but the bulge it created downright hurt, and now she could see that Matt was struggling not to laugh.

"It's not funny," she tried to say, but now he was laughing, and she was laughing too, not because this was the second time he'd caught her stuffing her face, but because all of this was different. And wrong. And if her mother were here, there would be no cheese biscuit crammed in her mouth at all. They'd all be seated, at the table, with napkins in their laps. Cloth napkins.

And because if she didn't laugh, she actually feared she might cry.

"Why don't I turn my back until you've finished?" Matt offered.

At that, she swatted him, and managed to get down the rest of the biscuit. That was it. She wasn't eating any more tonight, no matter how much Candy insisted that she did.

"I didn't know you would be here tonight," she said, not that she minded, she realized. Sure, Matt might not be someone she should pin her hopes to, but right now he was a distraction, and a positive one. And he was a reminder of the way things used to be, back before everything changed for the worse. Having him here, in her childhood home, felt good. Better than good. It felt comforting, stabilizing. And right. "Did Britt invite you?"

All of the Bradfords were here of course. She should have expected that Matt would come, too.

Still, she'd have words with Britt about that later. The least her sister could have done was tip her off! She could have borrowed another dress from Maddie. Done something with her hair. Fixed the chipped remnants of last weekend's manicure, when hope had felt so alive.

Now she felt no such hope. At least...she didn't dare to. But from the way Matt was looking her, intensely, as if there was something he wanted to say, she started to wonder if she had given up too soon.

Or if, maybe, she had a bit of cheese biscuit stuck to her mouth.

"Candy actually invited me." He grinned. Broadly. As if that was that.

And really, wasn't it?

"Ah, so you've met my father's girlfriend." Amelia suppressed a smile and nodded slowly.

"Oh yes. She was in town, passing out flyers, wanted me to vote for your café in some...contest?"

Amelia's eyes hooded. "She didn't."

The grin on Matt's face didn't slip. "Oh, she did. Actually, she stood and waited for me to log in to the voting site on my phone, and then she checked my vote for added measure."

Amelia's mouth went dry and it had nothing to do with Candy's cheese biscuit and everything to do with her behavior. "I am very sorry about that. I had no idea she was taking it upon herself to do that. I'll talk to her."

"If you do, you should tell her thank you! She's a real cheerleader for you." He gave her a wry smile.

Amelia felt her tension fade away. "I guess I'm lucky to have her in my corner. My dad is too." She stared down at her plate of food. His cholesterol was another matter...

"So what was this contest? To be honest, Candy was talking so quickly, I was half-expecting her to take my phone from my hand and just vote for me." He laughed, but Amelia still struggled to find this funny. She could only hope that the rest of the town was as patient as Matt.

Or as supportive of her business as she'd known them to always be.

"It's nothing," she said, shaking her head, even though, really, it was something, and now that she'd entered her recipe, photos, and a paragraph about what made Firefly so special, she couldn't help but think of how let down she'd be if she didn't win.

She looked at Matt, thinking about his meeting with the mayor and the fact that she still didn't know for certain how it went, though seeing as he was still in town, she had more reason to think that it had been a good meeting. Maybe even promising.

Maybe the mayor agreed with Matt. Felt change was necessary to carry Blue Harbor into the future. The council would have to put it to a vote, she knew, but the mayor held a lot of weight. With the right support, Matt would have his resort.

And then...Amelia didn't know. She supposed that she'd adjust, just as she always had. And truth be told, it might be nice to have Matt in town a little more often. If not permanently.

So long as her business was intact, she supposed that was really all she should worry about. And if she won the contest, she'd have bragging rights and added security.

"Didn't seem like nothing to Candy," Matt said, raising his eyebrows.

"Oh, she gets excited about everything," Amelia said. She wouldn't be pushed into discussing the contest. She'd learned not to set her hopes too high, especially when it was something that she cared about.

Like the man standing in front of her, she thought.

Note taken.

"It's a recipe contest, really," she said, even though it was oh so much more than that. She handed him the plate. "Here. Have a cheese biscuit. They're Candy's signature dish."

His eyes gleamed when he glanced down at the pile and back up at her. "You mean you don't want another?"

"No," she said firmly.

"But you must have at least six here. You were hungry." He cocked an eyebrow. His eyes positively shone.

She narrowed her gaze on him, just as Candy came swishing into the hallway. It was only then that Amelia did a double take at Candy's outfit. The apron she wore gave the distinct impression that there might not be any shirt beneath it, and she didn't know if she was relieved or horrified to realize that Candy was wearing a bright pink tube top with her white pants.

"So you came," Candy winked at Matt and gave Amelia a nudge with her elbow that could have easily toppled her over. Luckily, the banister was within short reach.

Candy didn't even notice. She was too busy roving her eyes over Matt, taking him in, even though she'd no doubt formed her opinion yesterday when she'd all but accosted him on the street.

"When I heard that Amelia's childhood sweetheart was back in town, well, I just had to make it my mission to find him!"

*Oh, please don't. Please, no.* Amelia hoped her gaze conveyed her silent pleas, but unlike her sisters would have been, Candy was oblivious.

She linked her arm with Matt, who gamely went along with it. His grin was positively wicked now.

"It isn't everyday that you have a second chance with your first love, now is it?" Candy didn't wait for a reply before adding, "And I just know that Amelia has been cooped up in that café and in desperate need for a man to get her out into the land of the living!"

Her heart lurched. "Well, now, Candy. I have dated—"

But Candy wasn't finished. "And what about you, Matt? You are single, right?"

Matt did his best to give the most serious nod. "Yes, Candy. I am unattached."

Now Candy looked at him suspiciously. "But you're not like your cousin Jackson, are you? You know, one of those guys who is determined to never settle down and experience the joy that can only come from the long-term love of a good woman?"

Now it was Amelia's turn to stifle a laugh. Matt looked as if he had swallowed one of Candy's famous cheese biscuits whole.

"I'd say I'm a little more like Robbie," Matt finally said, and Candy positively beamed as she turned to look at Amelia head on.

"You two have fun then," she said, giving Amelia a less than subtle wink.

"Well, I'm certainly having fun. Are you having fun?" Matt laughed as Candy disappeared into the dining room.

"Ha ha," Amelia said, but she was smiling for real now. "I'm sort of partied out, honestly."

"Are you suggesting that I take you out into the land of the living?" he asked, and before she could even swat him, his shoulders started shaking with laughter.

"She's sweet," he said, giving her a knowing look.

"Sweet? Or pushy?" Amelia dragged out a sigh.

Matt nodded to the door. "We could head out for a bit. Take a walk before the cake is cut?"

She held in a breath, knowing that her sisters would practically be pushing her out that front door rather than asking her to stay back. And Candy...Well, Candy would throw her out of the house if she could.

But Candy didn't have all the facts. And neither did her sisters.

And really, neither did she. She just knew that Matt had a vision that didn't match hers. But they shared a past. One that was comforting and familiar. One that had meant a great deal to her and still did.

Just like a part of him still did.

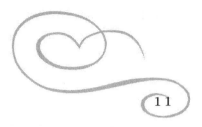

11

The party had spilled out onto the backyard, where friends and family had gathered at picnic tables and sat in Adirondack chairs overlooking the lake. Amelia knew that if she lingered too long that someone would be bound to spot her and call out to her, and then, another opportunity would be lost.

She was happy to see that Matt walked in the opposite direction of the yard, cutting through the yard of the house next door, which was a summer cottage and currently unoccupied by its now Florida resident owners—even though Amelia's father had been telling the neighbors for years that they should rent it out when they weren't visiting.

"Thanks," she said, once she had glanced over her shoulder and was certain that they were in the clear. The shore was rocky on this part of the coastline, and she expertly dodged the larger boulders as they walked along the natural terrain. "It was getting a little...overwhelming back there."

He studied her sidelong. "How so?"

Amelia sighed, not sure if she even wanted to get into it, but her heart was heavy and she knew that it would stay on her mind if she didn't speak up. And if there was anyone who might understand how she felt other than her sisters, it was Matt. He'd been there when her mother was alive, and he'd been there when she was gone.

And he'd now experienced the pleasure of not one but two encounters with Candy, and one was usually enough to form a strong opinion.

Despite herself, Amelia felt a smile pull at her frown.

"It's not easy being back in the house now that it's all...different." She glanced up at him, wondering if he would understand, and from the resigned look to his eyes, she knew that he did. "Every time I walk through the doors, or around a corner, I expect to see my mother, sitting in her favorite armchair, or standing at the kitchen counter, looking out the window. Her photos are still on the walls. Everything is really just like it always was in many ways. Except, it's not."

"Do you mean because of Candy?" Despite the sobering conversation, she caught the glimmer in his eyes.

She gave a little smile. "No. Yes. I mean, it's been different for a while. From the moment she was gone. Now I suppose it just feels more permanent. At least before, we still upheld our family traditions. Now Candy's putting a new spin on things."

"I think she wants you to like her," Matt said, giving her a lopsided grin.

"I know, and I do like her. It's just going to be an adjustment." She sighed. "Sometimes it feels like that's how it always is. One change after another. Don't you sometimes wish that you could just freeze time, and keep things exactly as they are for a while?"

She glanced up at him and their eyes locked for one telling moment, long enough to make her heart start to beat a little faster. She would freeze this moment, if she could. When it was just Matt and her, and the great big lake spread out before them, and everything felt like it should be. That she could trust him. That she knew him. That the world may keep changing, but that they were the same two people so long as they were together.

She looked away, pulling in a breath. "It sounds silly, probably. Here I am, thirty years old, and my mother has been gone for nearly half my life. You would think I'd be used to it by now."

"It's not that simple, I know," Matt said, his voice low and gentle.

Amelia felt the hot tears burn the backs of her eyes, and she blinked hard out onto the water. "You can't go back," she said quietly. "No matter how much you wish for it."

"No," Matt said, gruffly. "You can't."

She looked up at him, surprised by his sudden shift in tone, to see him staring out over the water, his jaw squared, his eyes focused on something other than Evening Island, she knew.

Finally, he said, "It wasn't easy for me to go back into my house the other day either."

Amelia closed her eyes, feeling bad for her part in it, and set a hand on his arm. Damn. It felt good. His skin was warm under her palm, and soft, familiar, and she wanted to stay like this, just for a little while, only she wasn't sure that it was her place anymore. Or if he even wanted that.

"I'm sorry," she said. "I didn't mean to upset you. I just..." Well, she'd been trying to convince him of something she wanted. Something he had once wanted, too.

But that was a long time ago, and it was easy to lose sight of all the years that had gone by. Too easy.

He shook his head, brushing off her concern, and she let her arm drop. "It's fine. Really. I needed to see it eventually, and I probably would have gone by at some point on my visit out of curiosity. And it might have been worse if it was full of someone else's furniture and family photos."

Amelia understood that all too well. "That's how it feels with Candy, I suppose. She's a good person. Kind-hearted. She has the best intentions, and I know you're right that she just wants us to like her. She makes my dad really happy." She was trying to convince herself, she knew. She could hear the insistence in her tone, trying to tell her that she had no reason to feel so conflicted about this woman as she did.

"But she's not your mother," Matt observed.

"Exactly," Amelia said quietly. Her sandals were growing muddy, so she stopped to remove them. The water was cold as it splashed over her toes, but she didn't mind it. It reminded her of all those happy, summer days, when she stood barefoot in this sand, staring out over the lake. Days filled with her mother, her sisters.

And later, with Matt.

She looked over at him, catching the pensive knit of his brow, the way his hair rustled in the breeze, and even though more than twelve years had passed since they had both stood like this, side by side, facing the water, it felt like no time had gone by at all. That she was still the same girl she had been back then: heartbroken, a little lost, determined to get through each day as best she could because she didn't know what alternative there was.

Maybe, she thought, he was still the same boy.

Or maybe, that was just wishful thinking.

"You asked me the other day if I had ever thought about leaving Blue Harbor," she said. "And the truth of it is that I did. Sometimes. I mean, it's a small town, and I've lived here all my life. I thought about going somewhere else, just for a change of scenery."

"You have family here," he said.

She nodded. "Yes, but...maybe it was just an easy excuse, you know? It's not easy to go out into the world and try something new. I give you a lot of credit for that, Matt. It couldn't have been easy to start over, halfway through your senior year of high school, in a city where you didn't know anyone."

He pulled in a breath, growing quiet for a moment. "It was pretty damn hard," he said with a small smile, but there was sadness in his eyes, something that looked an awful lot like pain.

He picked up a rock and skipped it over the surface of the water. It was a skill she'd never been able to master, despite hours upon hours of trying in her lifetime.

"To be honest, though, it was just as hard to come back here."

She looked at him in surprise. His eyes were fixed on the water, or something in the distance. Or maybe a memory. Something she hadn't been a part of.

"But you had family here, too. And friends." *And me*, she thought to herself. She'd been here all this time.

"It wasn't the same. No one could understand. Not even my cousins or aunt and uncle."

She couldn't help but feel hurt by his words. "Not even me?" She stared at him, challenging him, until he met her gaze, his expression reluctant. "I might have understood. I still can."

He hesitated for a moment and then shook his head. "I loved this town. I loved my life. And then, one day, it was gone. The house was being foreclosed on and the business was gone and my parents were arguing all the time and my mom was always crying. And then we had to pack up and leave. And everyone else got to stay. And I was angry. I was so angry. Angry at my parents. Angry at the new school and having to be there. Angry that my dad lost his business."

She nodded slowly. She understood. It was how she felt when her mom got sick. How she felt in those long, dark weeks and months after her mother was gone, when she saw other classmates shopping in town with their mothers. She stopped going to friends' homes, because it hurt too much to see their mothers welcome her inside, always with a touch more kindness than before, but still, a reminder that when she went home she would not find her mother there with a tired smile after a long day. She'd thrown herself into her home life, into the comfort of a routine, and she'd held onto Matt, the bright spot in a dark time.

"You know that everyone wanted you to stay. They wished they could have helped your family. They missed you." She paused. "I missed you."

His gaze was intense, and she looked away, down at her feet, at the pebbles surrounding her toes. She picked one up, even though it was hopeless, because despite everything, there was always some small reserve in her heart that this time, things might be different. Better.

"I never forgot how it felt to leave this town," Matt said. "I wanted to come back. But I didn't want to come back feeling like I did when I left. Like an outsider."

She shook her head. "You're one of us. You swam in this lake. You rode your bike on these paths. You know this town."

And that was why she couldn't understand why he was hell-bent on seeing that design come to life.

Except...that maybe she could. Because it was a solution. An answer. Because he didn't believe in throwing the same rock out into the water waiting for a different result. Matt thought that the way to keep a business alive in this town was to do something that hadn't been done.

That hadn't failed.

*

Matt picked up another stone and skipped it across the water. It was a favorite pastime as a kid, seeing how many skips he could get, keeping a running tally with his brother and cousins. He usually won.

"I haven't skipped stones since I lived here," he said, marveling at that. "It never gets old."

Beside him, Amelia shrugged. "Some things don't. I guess it's another reason that I decided to stay in town. Sure, it's far from exciting, but it's home. The good memories and the bad ones. It's my life."

He pulled in a breath. Now was as good a time as any to talk to her about the café, he knew. To feel her out, to warn her. Maybe he had nothing to worry about. Maybe she would see that her business would do better if it had more street traffic. Amelia was sensible, and she was clearly a good businesswoman.

"It's one of the reasons I bought the café, actually," she said, cutting him off before he could release the words from the back of his throat.

He swallowed hard and stared at her. "What do you mean?"

"That café is like my second home. It's where my mother would take us after school a few days a week, to have a hot drink, and maybe a cookie, to talk about our days. Putting the money she left me into buying it just made me feel like she was still with me. My father always advised us to hold onto our shares, telling us we would know exactly what to do with it when the time came. I honestly felt like my mother was looking down on me the day that Dorothy decided to sell." She laughed. "You know, it was actually at that café that I first told my mother about you."

"About me?" He stared at her in surprise. "But we've known each other all our lives."

"Right, but I mean...when I started seeing things in a different light..." Her cheeks turned pink when she caught his eye. "I remember telling my mom about it, right at the corner table. The one near the patio doors?" She grinned until her eyes turned distant. "That was a good day."

Now Matt was curious, and despite himself, he was eager to know more. "Well, don't leave me hanging like that. What did you tell her?"

She looked at him. "That was like...fifteen years ago. And you know how it all turned out."

He poked her in the waist. She laughed, inched away, but her gaze lingered for a second longer than normal when she looked his way again.

"I said that I thought you would be the man I would marry."

She glanced away at the omission and tossed the rock in her hand into the water. It sunk directly to the bottom.

"Anyway," she said, unable to look him in the eye. "Obviously that didn't happen."

No, it hadn't, Matt thought. It might have, if circumstances had been different. Still, neither one of them were married. Not that Amelia would be speaking to him for much longer if the town insisted the resort be built on the spot that currently housed her café rather than the parcel he'd chosen.

"That café has a lot of sentimental value for you," he said. It wasn't just business to Amelia. She may look practical and fastidious, but underneath it all, she was all heart. He'd always loved that about her.

Still did, if he was being honest with himself.

*

Amelia didn't know why she was going on like this. Really, she started to wonder if Candy's cheese biscuits were spiked with beer or something—if that was what made them so special in Candy's eye.

But she knew that it was nothing like that. She'd always had an easy way when it came to Matt.

Good to know that this hadn't changed.

"I know I said that my biggest regret was leaving this town," Matt said, looking at her sidelong. His brow was pulled into a frown, his gaze unwavering. "But the truth is that my biggest regret was not keeping in touch with the people in this town. With my cousins. And especially, with you."

Amelia pulled in a breath, pushing back the hope that filled her chest as her heart began to pound. "I understand now, Matt. It wasn't easy for you to leave. And sometimes...it's more painful to try to hold on than to let something go."

He nodded, but his expression showed that he wasn't convinced. "I wanted to call or write or visit, every day. And not just that senior year. Every day after that. I was going through the motions. Living my life. But a part of me...Well, it was always here." He gave a little smile. "That's why it was so important for me to get back."

"For closure?" She blinked up at him as he turned to face her properly. He was close, very close, close enough for her to see the flecks of green in his otherwise blue eyes. To feel the urge to reach out, sense the heat of his skin just one more time.

"Maybe," he said. "Or maybe, I was just holding out hope, that if I came back, it would be different, and it wouldn't have to end like it did before."

She nodded, unable to say anything, because now he was close, and his eyes were so intense, so familiar in their hold on hers, that she knew that he might just kiss her again, and that this time, she would let him.

He leaned in, slowly, slow enough for her to clear her throat, take a step back, tell herself that this was a bad idea, and that he wasn't the boy she had once loved with all her heart.

Only standing here, like this, she believed that he was. His intentions may have been misplaced somewhere along the way, but his heart was right here in Blue Harbor. Where it had always been.

Where hers would always be.

His lips were soft and gentle when they met hers, but his hold on her was firm and strong. He pulled her close against his chest, his arms wrapped fully around her waist as he drew her near, and all the sounds around them seemed to fade away as she leaned in and experienced his warmth.

Finally, she broke away, looking up at him with a pounding heart. His eyes were intense, and her mind was racing, with possibility, with confusion, and more than anything...with hope.

Now wasn't the time to worry about when he was going back to Minneapolis or what his intentions were. Now was the time to just be together, as they had once been.

"I should probably get back to the party before they sing the birthday song. I'd hate to disappoint my sister," she said.

Although something told her that if Britt had any idea that she had just kissed Matt Bradford, she'd find it in her heart to forgive her.

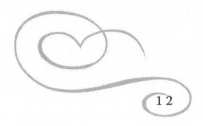

12

Matt woke the next morning to the smell of toast and eggs—Jackson's signature breakfast when one of them didn't pick up bagels in Pine Falls.

Usually, Matt's stomach grumbled at the promise of a meal hot and waiting, but today he lingered in the guest room, tired from a restless night.

He'd gone and kissed Amelia Conway. Kissed her because he wanted to, because she was right there, looking at him, so beautiful and so close, and standing there, talking to her, had made him feel good. Better than good. It had filled a part of him that had been missing for so many years, something he thought he was filling by coming back to town now, with a plan in place.

This wasn't part of the plan. And instead of telling Amelia the truth, or warning her, he had gone and kissed her.

He threw on a tee shirt and opened the door. The hallway was short and he could see Jackson standing at the counter in the kitchen, already plating their food that they would no doubt take over to the sofa to eat. Jackson had a dining table, but Matt very much suspected that, like his own, it was underused. A few candlelit dinners that never went anywhere. The occasional need for a desk when the real one was cluttered.

They were two bachelors, getting by. Not much different than the kids they had once been.

Matt's mind wandered back to last night again.

Not much different at all.

He grabbed a mug from the cabinet and filled it with coffee. Jackson was already digging into his scrambled eggs, not bothering to sit on a stool. He was watching Matt carefully, as if waiting for the right opportunity to say something that was on his mind.

For one fleeting second, Matt wondered if he'd gotten wind of the mayor's proposal for the location of his resort. It was a small town. It was entirely possible.

Which was why he should have come clean with Amelia last night when he had the chance, rather than kissing her like that.

Still, if he had it all to do over again, he couldn't say that he wouldn't have made the same choice all over again. Kissing Amelia felt just as good now as it had back then. Only just like back then, he had the horrible feeling that it was all about to come to an end.

"You went to bed right when you got back last night," Jackson said. "I didn't even have a chance to ask where you and Amelia disappeared to during the party."

Matt opened his mouth to deny the accusation, but one look at Jackson's amused expression told him there was no point. "Think anyone else noticed?"

Jackson seemed to consider this while he took a bite from the corner of his toast. "Probably not. I guess it's a professional hazard. I'm used to watching a crowd. And you and Amelia were missing from it for quite some time."

Matt slid his plate across the counter. "We went for a walk."

"And?" Jackson raised an eyebrow, clearly not believing that this was all there was to the story.

Matt saw his blueprints and files spread out on the buffet table, his mind drifting away back to reality. He'd discussed the project with his cousins, but not in detail. Now, he was eager to see Jackson's thoughts on his design. He respected the guy. Always had. Looked up to him, even. Jackson had always been confident and self-assured, no matter what life threw his way. He was easygoing, and above all, he was honest.

And Matt needed some brutal honesty right now. Really, he needed to be honest with himself.

"Change of subject," he started but Jackson let out a groan of protest.

"Oh no, if you think I'm going to let you off the hook that easy, try again." He folded his arms across his chest, waiting. "Go on. What happened?"

"What do you think happened?" Matt replied, and Jackson let out a low whistle.

There was no hiding his smile when he said, "You always had a soft spot for Amelia Conway. Think you guys have a chance of getting back together?"

Probably not once Amelia found out about the proposed location of his design, Matt thought.

He shrugged and forced some eggs into his mouth, even though his throat felt tight. This Friday was the town council meeting. Next weekend he was scheduled to return to Minneapolis. And then what? He hadn't come to Blue Harbor with any expectations for getting back together with his high school girlfriend. He'd just come to town with the hope of feeling better than he had when he'd left it.

And he had felt better. Until now.

"Amelia's not a fan of my work," he said. He walked to the buffet and began unrolling his blueprints. He spread them out on the island, careful not to get too close to the breakfast plates. "Be honest."

Jackson considered the paper silently. "It's certainly different," he finally said. He took a long sip of his coffee, narrowing his eyes on Matt. "Guess I won't have to worry about losing business at the inn."

"It would certainly be a different market," Matt agreed. Now, looking at the design he had spent so much time finalizing, he could almost see it through Amelia's eyes. It was cold, and it didn't fit in with the rest of the buildings in town. Sure, it might have worked out at the edge of town, hidden by the tall trees from the forest, but did it deserve a spot just behind Main Street, in the heart of town?

He wanted to believe that it did, but deep down, in his gut, he knew it didn't.

And the last thing he wanted was to have more regrets when it came to this town.

He rolled up the papers, pushing aside the knots that were building in his stomach. Everything had seemed so clear when he'd first returned to Blue Harbor. And somewhere along the way the plan had veered off course, and not just because of the mayor's insistence of the new location.

Because of Amelia. And his feelings for her. And that kiss.

Matt stared out the window onto the large body of water. Once, he had imagined guests at his hotel taking in this very same view. Now, it no longer excited him as it should. Instead it left him with a strange feeling in his gut. One of discomfort. One not much different from the way he'd felt when his parents had told him they were leaving Blue Harbor.

"I think I'll take a walk."

Jackson was refilling his mug with coffee at the counter. "Want me to join you?"

Matt shook his head. He needed to be alone, to think. And he knew if he told Jackson what was running through his head that Jackson would tell him what he already knew, deep down.

He just wasn't sure if he was ready to listen to it yet.

"I need to make some calls back to the office. I won't be gone long."

Jackson shrugged and took his coffee into the living room, where he collapsed on the leather armchair and flicked on the news.

Matt stepped out onto the back porch and breathed in the smells around him. The air was so clear here, it filled his lungs effortlessly. In the distance he could hear the call of birds, the lapping of the gentle waves that rocked Jackson's boat.

Life was simple here. Easy. And peaceful. And that was what pulled people to it. It was escape from the hustle and noise of life in the city or other denser environments. Here, time slowed down, allowed you to think. Allowed your mind to drift to the past.

For so long he'd been focused on the future.

Now, he wasn't even sure what it held.

He pulled his phone from his pocket and circled back toward the house until he had a strong signal. Bob answered on the third ring. In the background, Matt could hear the usual din of the office. The muffled sound of people talking, the whir of the printer. The clacking of computer keys.

He didn't miss any of it. And somehow, getting a bigger position in that same office left him even emptier than he'd been before.

"We might have a problem," he told Bob, clenching his free hand at his side.

There was a beat of silence. "What kind of a problem?"

"That land we discussed? The mayor won't have it."

Bob cursed under his breath. "I had a feeling that would be a problem. I'll get to work on some other site selections."

"No need," Matt said. He stared out onto the water. Wondered if he could really say what he wanted to say. "There's a stretch along the waterfront that they're proposing. They've been wanting to put the land to better use."

"Excellent!" Bob said, as if that solved all their problems.

If only it did.

"The problem is that I don't like that site," Matt said. There was silence on the other end of the line. "I don't think it's the right fit."

And it wasn't. Not for Amelia. Not for him. And not for the project, though he could make it work. A week ago he would have jumped at the chance to make it work.

"Don't tell me you're having doubts," Bob said, his tone incredulous.

"Of course I'm not having doubts!" Matt shot back, his voice rising in defense.

"Good, because you didn't spend all this time coming up with a design just to bail on it at the final hour. And I didn't spend months pulling demographic research to back up your case for the development team for nothing."

There was a pause, and Matt knew it was his turn to speak, but he couldn't think of anything to say.

"I'm not having doubts." He wasn't. Not entirely. He had worked too hard, and not just to come up with the design, to make it airtight, a slam dunk, but had worked too hard through college, and the years working up the corporate ladder, just to get back to Blue Harbor.

Only to turn around and leave it again.

He pushed that thought back. Told himself that bringing the development to town would be closure. That it would allow him to visit with a less heavy heart from now on. That he'd have a reason to return, and that he'd feel good when he did.

Only he would still be just visiting. Just passing through. An outsider, rather than a member of this community that he had loved and cherished.

And missed.

\*

Amelia was in the café, prepping for the next day, when the bells above the door jingled.

Damn. She must have forgotten to lock it behind her. Even though the "Closed" sign was turned, it didn't necessarily stop people from wandering in and asking for a cup of coffee. She sighed and set her list down on the kitchen island, then pushed out into the dining room

Candy was standing near the door, her eyes frantic, and her hair wild—the curls frizzy and the roots wet.

Amelia looked outside. Sure enough, it had started to drizzle. Maybe Candy had slipped inside to get out of the rain. She wouldn't blame her. She'd even offer her a cup of coffee. She could use one herself. She'd barely slept last night, thinking about that kiss. Playing it over, and over, and wondering what it meant. And where it might lead.

"Candy!" She smiled. "If I didn't say it last night, that was a really nice party."

Candy, for once, was not smiling. She lunged forward and grabbed Amelia by the wrists, squeezing hard. "I'm not entirely sure it was so nice. I'm told that there was some nefarious business going on right under my nose!"

Amelia peered at her. "Nefarious business?"

"That Matthew Bradford!"

Amelia felt her cheeks flush. So perhaps they hadn't slipped away unnoticed as she'd hoped. And perhaps when they'd returned to the party, it had been noticeable, along with their shared absence.

"Oh," she said. "That." She pulled her hands free and went behind the counter to start a fresh pot of coffee. She would have thought Candy would be happy to know that she and Matt were...She pulled in a breath and released a happy sigh.

"Yes. That!" Candy looked most put out. "You know he has terrible plans for this town, Amelia!"

"Well, now I wouldn't call them *terrible*," Amelia said, feeling a little bad that she had implied such a thing to Matt when he'd first shown her the rendering. "And it's entirely possible that the town council won't vote it through."

"Well, I should hope not!" Candy scoffed. "I assume you'll be there, to speak against it! I'm calling on all local business owners to do that." This was quite a statement, considering that Candy was not a business owner. But then, Amelia's father was, technically.

Amelia turned from the coffee machine and looked at Candy. "Don't you think that's taking things a little far? Sure, it wouldn't be my choice, but I don't really feel I have much say in the matter. And he raised a very good point that this resort could be good for the town."

And maybe, it would be good for her, too. She'd adapted to change before, and this kind of change could bring Matt back to town for longer than his current stay.

Candy blinked at her, her mouth a perfect oval. "Amelia Conway! I cannot even believe my ears! That man intends to tear down this lovely café of yours and you don't plan to stop him?"

Amelia felt the blood drain from her face. "What do you mean, he intends to tear down this café?" She spoke slowly, but her mind was in overdrive as she tried to play through the details of her conversation with Matt. "He said he wanted to plan it for the other side of the beach. Over near the cliff."

"Well, that's not what I'm told." Candy folded her arms across her chest with a huff. "I was over at the town hall today, getting more votes for your contest entry, and I happened to get into a conversation with the assistant to the mayor."

Amelia raised her eyebrow. *Happened* to was probably a stretch.

"As soon as she heard me mention your café, she asked me how you felt about moving up to Main Street. Well, needless to say, I had no idea what she was talking about!"

Main Street. Was that what Matt had been getting at the other night when he'd asked her about the location of her business?

"I own this half of the building," Amelia said. "They can't just make me leave."

Candy pinched her lips. "The other businesses along this path are all too happy to sell, and with the space next door being empty, that just leaves you."

Amelia's mind raced. "They can't force me out?"

"Apparently, they can!" Candy looked mad enough to punch something.

Amelia's hands were shaking when she reached for a mug, and she set it back down.

Candy brushed past her and took her by the shoulders, led her over to a seat near the window. It was the very seat she had sat in with her mother all those years ago. Back when life felt full of so much hope and possibility. Back when Matt felt like a glimpse into her future, not a look back at her past.

Candy reappeared a moment later with two steaming mugs.

Amelia gripped one in her hands, letting it warm her skin. Even though it was August, she suddenly felt cold.

"Tell me everything, Candy, because I still don't think I understand what you're saying." Only she did. She just wished it was a misunderstanding.

Candy pursed her lips. Her nostrils flared slightly. She took a big breath: energy for what was to come.

"Martha and I go way back. She lives right on the town line between Blue Harbor and Pine Falls. Believe it or not, I actually used to babysit her when I was younger. Now, I know, I know, you are probably wondering how on earth that was possible, given how young I look..."

Martha was somewhere in her early forties. And Candy...Well, Candy was dating Amelia's father.

"I was a very young babysitter," Candy went on as she added spoonful after spoonful of sugar to her coffee absentmindedly. "Very trusted. Always good with the little ones." She beamed.

Amelia dipped her chin. "Candy. What happened?"

Candy gave a little start, and then cleared her throat and set down her spoon. She straightened her shoulders, giving Amelia a long, hard look. "That young man has bad intentions, Amelia. You know I have your best intentions at heart, but I'm sorry to say, I can't be sure that I can say that same for Matt Bradford."

Amelia stared out the window, shaking her head. "I can't believe this. This café means everything to me."

"We have to fight!" Candy said firmly. "If we have to, we'll tie ourselves to that tree out there." She flicked her chin to the big maple. "I'll chain myself to your front door if it comes down to it."

Despite the conversation, Amelia felt her heart warm. "Thank you, Candy, but...this is something I need to sort out for myself. I...need to run out for a bit." She didn't need to hear anymore. She'd heard enough. And she knew that Candy meant every word that she had said. She did have the best intentions for her—for all of them.

Just like Matt had said, she thought, narrowing her eyes.

"But it's raining!" Candy said in alarm.

A little rain didn't matter right now, and it wasn't going to stop her either.

She needed to find Matt. She needed to hear him say it, right to her face. And then... Then she didn't even know anymore.

Matt Bradford had come back to town and turned everything upside down.

Including her heart.

*

Amelia tried Jackson's house first, even though it was all the way on the edge of town. She knocked on the door, knowing that it was early enough in the day that Jackson might still be home if Matt wasn't. But no answer came, and when she looked through the windows, she could see that it was dark and still inside.

She hopped on her bike, maneuvering it over the increasingly muddy path, trying to avoid the puddles. If she'd been thinking more clearly she would have brought her car. But she wasn't thinking clearly. Her mind kept snapping back and forth from the memory of that kiss to the words that Candy had spoken.

She pedaled faster, ducking her head against the falling rain, and headed back into town. Matt wouldn't be outside. Not on a day like this. And that left only a few places in town. The inn, which his aunt and uncle owned. Maybe he and Jackson were having a bite at the pub. Or maybe...

She pulled in a breath and circled back around to the building at the far end of Main Street. Like so many others, it was wood sided, only instead of being painted white, it was red, with crisp black shutters. The town library had always been a sanctuary for Matt, after school, and she'd often meet him there. He liked to pour over the big, hardbound books that showed photographs of buildings all across the world. He wanted to travel. He wanted to see everything.

But he didn't want to leave Blue Harbor. It was clear back then. And it was clear last night.

She parked her bike at the medal stand alongside a few others and hurried into the building, which was warmly lit by sconces and lamps. The floors were scuffed, covered in fading rugs, and the tables were dark wood. At the front desk was Helena, the town librarian who had once been a classmate of Amelia's.

And Matt's.

Amelia's heart stalled as she approached the counter, where Helena seemed to be taking great pride in tallying up late fees.

Helena tutted when she saw Amelia approach. "You have to tell your stepmother to stop checking out so many of those romance novels. She has a late fee on fifteen of them!"

Amelia pulled in a breath. She knew that Candy devoured those books. Britt even heard her reading them allowed to their father before he got the arm cast removed and could finally pick up his own books again.

"She's not my stepmother," she corrected. But that was the least of her problems at the moment. She darted her eyes to the room on either side of the lobby and lowered her voice. "Listen, have you by any chance seen Matt come through?"

Now Helena looked up at her with interest. "Matt *Bradford*?" She blinked, letting this soak in. A smiled curved her mouth when she leaned forward, speaking in a low whisper she had mastered over the years. "I didn't know he was back in town. Are you two...?" She waggled her eyebrows, and Amelia shook her head, forcefully.

"No. I mean... No." Only yesterday, if Helena had asked her the same question, she might have said yes. And she wanted to say yes. Nearly as much as she wanted to believe that Candy had just gotten mixed up, or misplaced the truth somewhere along with the library books.

But if there was one thing she had learned over the past few years, it was that her family had her back. And Candy was part of the family now.

"Honestly, I've been so busy sending out these bills that I haven't picked my head up for a few minutes. He might have come through. I was busy with story time earlier..." Helena opened her eyes wide and shrugged.

"Thanks, Helena. I'll just take a look-see." Amelia pursed her lips at the bill spread out on the counter. She dug around in her purse until she found her overstuffed wallet, full of receipts she still had to enter into her spreadsheets for her accountant. "Let me cover Candy's late fees." It was the least she could do for the woman, after all, considering that Candy might be chaining herself to a tree at this very moment.

With that settled, she began walking through the rooms of the library. It still smelled the same as it always had, a little musty, even a little dusty, though she knew that Helena ran a tight ship and kept things clean and tidy. She went positively pale if she saw a book shelved incorrectly.

The rain pattered against the long windows that framed the rooms along the perimeter, and Amelia did a round, darting her head between shelves, before deciding to go downstairs, just to be sure.

She never went down there. Never had need. It was where all the town records were housed, because there wasn't enough storage at the neighboring town hall.

And that was where she saw him, standing over a table, a map of downtown Blue Harbor spread in front of him.

Guilty as charged.

He looked up, startled to sense someone behind him, and his expression changed from surprise, to pleasure, to concern, to knowing, all in a matter of seconds.

Yep. Guilty.

"Tell me it isn't true," she said, but her voice caught in her throat. She was shaking, and not just because she was half wet from the long bike ride over here. She didn't want to hear the truth any more than she knew she needed to hear it.

His shoulders sagged as he released a breath, telling her everything she needed to know.

"How could you?" She shook her head bitterly. "You knew what that café meant to me!"

"No," he said firmly. He stepped toward her, but she took a step back. She set a hand on the banister railing to steady herself. "I swear, Amelia. I didn't know until last night just why that café meant so much. You have to believe me that this was never my plan."

"So you're going to tell me that standing here, studying that map isn't all part of your grand plan?"

"It is. But...it's not what it looks like." His eyes pleaded with hers, but he said nothing more for a moment, just shook his head, set his jaw. "You have no idea what it took for me to come back here, Amelia. I wanted to make things right."

"Well, you got it all wrong," she said scornfully. "And now it looks like all that anger has finally found an outlet. You never got over what happened all those years ago, you were angry, and jealous, and now you're bringing us all down with you."

"That's not fair, Amelia." He flashed her a warning glance, one that went straight to her chest, but she too was too angry to apologize right now.

"My parents lost their business."

"And now I lose mine?" She stared at him.

"It wasn't my idea," he said. "It wasn't what I wanted. But you don't have to lose your business, Amelia. You might do better on Main Street!"

She closed her eyes, shaking her head. "You don't get it. It's not about a big profit to me. It's not about that to any of these businesses in town, and it wasn't about that to your parents either. It's about community. About traditions. About pulling together when times are tough, not tearing each other down. You know that Robbie and Jackson's parents tried to help your father. But he didn't want their help."

Matt blinked. His eyes looked hollow as he stared at her. "What do you mean?"

"People pitched in. They knew the business was struggling, but they wanted to help get it over the hump. Wanted to help it succeed. Your father wanted to do it on his own."

Matt was quiet, too quiet, and she knew she'd hit a nerve. It was a truth that was long discussed, after Matt's family had left town, when the rift between the brothers seemed to be permanent, and when Bonnie Bradford lamented over losing her sister-in-law and dearest friend.

"Why are you looking at that map of Blue Harbor, Matt?" Her voice was almost a whisper, choked with fear of what he might say, even though she needed to hear it. No more hoping for the best or pushing aside her concerns. No more fooling herself. Or being made a fool of, for that matter.

He closed his eyes for the briefest of seconds. "I'm looking for alternate sites."

She knew that there weren't any. The town was built up, and the open space was meant to stay that way.

"And if you don't find any?"

His lips thinned. "Amelia, this isn't personal."

"You're wrong, Matt. This is personal. This town is personal. That café is personal. That..." She almost didn't say it. "That kiss was personal."

She shook her head, backing away.

"But you're right about one thing," she said, shaking her head. "You don't belong in this town."

Tears blinded her eyes and she turned and hurried up the steps before he could see them fall. She wanted to run, down the street, through town, and all the way home. But not to the home she shared with her sister. To her childhood home, the one she'd shared with her mother.

She felt lost, and scared, like a part of her was being taken away forever and she didn't know how she'd get through it. She'd felt like this once before, when her mother had left this earth. And that day she'd run straight to Matt.

The one person she couldn't turn to now.

13

Amelia never tired of coming into her café each day. Never grew bored of the view of the fishing boats bobbing on the water, or the brightly colored sails dotting the horizon. She loved the counter, lined with glass-dome covered cake stands that were piled high with the daily dessert offerings or quick breakfast options. She loved working in her kitchen, planning new recipes, and she loved walking through the dining room, greeting the patrons.

The tourists were her bread and butter, sure. But the locals...they were her family.

She wondered how they would feel about this place being torn down. If they would miss the back deck or the scuffed floorboards, or remember how it used to be, back when Dorothy still owned the place. She wondered if they held onto the memories the way that she did, or if it was just something replaceable to them. Maybe that would be best. She'd need their support at a new location if she intended to stay in business.

By Thursday morning, Amelia did feel tired. Not of her café, but from putting on a smile, going through the motions, pretending as if nothing were amiss when her heart felt like it was breaking. On the walk home the night before, she'd forced herself to stroll down Main Street, and consider her slim options, but she'd grown immediately anxious and upset, and hurried home where a batch of fresh ice cream was waiting for her in the freezer.

Now, as she turned the key to the front door of the café and flicked on the lights, she felt herself tear up at the sight. There, on the far wall, she'd hung a photo of her mother, standing in her apron. It was the first personal belonging she'd brought to the café when she'd first taken over it nearly six years ago. And there, on each table, was a votive candle in a small globe of sand and pebbles—she loved creating a small bit of seasonal decoration, especially during the holidays. Her blackboard still bore the specials from yesterday, and she yearned to feel the usual excitement to erase them and write today's specials. Now, she wasn't even sure there was much point. By tomorrow, her fate would be sealed.

With a heavy heart, she walked around the counter and into the kitchen, startling at the sight of all of her sisters, gathered around the work station.

"What are you all doing here?" she asked, her eyes flitting from one sister to the next.

"We're here to cheer you up," Britt said. She reached into her bag and revealed two bottles of wine. The newest blend. "I brought spirits."

"And I brought flowers," Cora said, handing over a beautiful cherry blossom wreath that Amelia could nearly imagine hanging on the door to the café. Or maybe, it would be better suited for the door to her home.

"And I brought pie." Maddie held out a large, lattice crust pie that smelled as if it were fresh from the oven and probably was.

Amelia forced a smile. Her sisters were trying. The least she could do was show her appreciation.

"I wish I could enjoy it all, but I have to get started on breakfast," she said. For today, at least, she thought darkly.

Maddie caught her frown and said loudly, "No need! I've already prepped everything, and the quiches just need to be popped in the oven. And one glass of wine won't kill you, even at this hour. You practically grew up on this stuff."

Amelia had to laugh at that. "Grew up around it," she said, but it was true that her father did let them taste test as they got older—small mouthfuls, but still. She could hold her own.

"One glass," she said. Yes, it was barely past sunrise, and she had a long day ahead of her, on her feet no less, but she could use a little something to take the edge off. And like Maddie said, one glass wouldn't kill her.

But losing this café just might.

"Wine before coffee." Britt uncorked a bottle. "Maybe I could do something with this..." Her eyes narrowed in thought.

The rest of them laughed. Some things would never change. Amelia supposed that there was comfort in that.

Maddie sliced the pie and doled it out and then Britt held up her glass in toast.

"Oh..." Amelia shook her head. "There's nothing to toast, Britt. I'm going to lose my café. "

"All thanks to Matt Bradford," Cora said scathingly. "I still can't even believe it."

None of them could. Maddie had been the one Amelia told, when she'd run home from the library, and it was Maddie who had told everyone else—that was, the ones that Candy hadn't already gotten to, and that was half the town.

"I'm disappointed," Britt said. "I can understand wanting to have a successful business, but this isn't the way. Matt isn't thinking of the town at all. He's just thinking of himself."

"Well, he certainly isn't thinking about me," Amelia said.

Britt looked at her sadly. "And here I thought something might be developing between you two again. At the concert, you seemed so connected. I thought something was still there."

"Me too," said Maddie.

"Me too," admitted Amelia.

The room fell silent. Then, Britt lifted her glass again, and despite Amelia's protests, insisted, "One toast. For this café. And for hope, that there is still a chance for it after all. A second chance. Because we all deserve one of those, even if it's not meant to be in the romance department."

She winked at Amelia, and despite her reservations, Amelia felt her shoulders relax. "I can toast to that."

"We all can," said Cora.

They clinked glasses, and each took a long sip.

"I think I'll make coffee too," Maddie said slowly, and they all started to laugh.

Still, there was a heaviness to the air as they each ate their pie and waited for the coffee to finish percolating.

"Well, in brighter news, the contest winner is revealed tomorrow!" Maddie looked around with wide eyes, trying to drum up some excitement.

Amelia had remembered that, somewhere in the back of her mind, like a grain of hope that hadn't yet been pulled out by the tide.

"It doesn't matter anymore," she said, dragging her fork through the pie filling.

"It certainly does matter!" Britt said. "Besides, if the winner is announced before the town council meeting, it will only reinforce your case."

Amelia knew her sisters were trying to give her hope, but now was the time for reality. She shook her head and pushed the plate away.

"It won't matter. The space next door has been vacant for months. The other stores along this path have been struggling for ages and will happily sell. And the bike shop has wanted to move to Main Street forever, they just couldn't afford it before. Do you really think they'll let me stay here just because I win some contest?" She shook her head. "Matt was right. That resort will bring a lot of business to the town. A lot of revenue. And what do I bring?"

Cora reached out a hand and set it over Amelia's. "You bring people together, Amelia. More than any of those pubs or restaurants on Main Street. This is a local place. This is a family place. And we're not letting it go without a fight."

Amelia felt the tears begin to burn the back of her eyes, and she sniffed against them. She wasn't sure if she was crying about the café or the disappointment that Matt had been the one to take it from her.

But it was more than that, she knew. She loved him. Then. Now. She loved him. She just didn't know him anymore.

"How could he do this?" She stared at her sisters, looking for answers that she knew none of them could give.

It was Britt who spoke. "Robbie isn't happy about it, either. Or Jackson. I guess they've been arguing."

Amelia didn't want to infer meaning that wasn't there. "Arguing must mean that Matt is holding firm."

Britt shook her head, looking dismayed. "He's changed, Amelia. Everyone's disappointed."

"But not everyone will lose their business," Amelia replied.

"We'll rebuild," Britt announced. "We'll make a fresh start. We've had a lot of experience with those."

"A lot of setbacks, you mean," Amelia said. She frowned, deeply.

"And we've always come out on top," Maddie said. She elbowed her gently, giving her a little smile. "It's going to be okay, Amelia. You still have us."

It was true. She still had her sisters. And she could still have a café. And this building, this view, these tables and windows and layout, and floorboards—they were just a structure. A house of memories. She had many of those.

"I'm just tired of losing things," she said softly.

"Are you talking about the café, or are you talking about Matt?" Britt was watching her, her face expressionless, free of judgment.

"Both," she admitted.

*

Matt sat on the old swing on the back of his childhood home, listening to the creaking of the chain with each inch that he moved. He probably shouldn't be here, but he doubted anyone would know, and those that might notice weren't likely to say anything. He'd lived here for eighteen years. Fallen down those stairs to the yard more times than he could count. Still had a scar on his knee to prove it.

Amelia's words echoed in his head, replaying over and over, like a song he couldn't stop hearing. It taunted him, but he knew that wasn't her intention. She was trying to show him that it didn't have to be this way. Not now. Not then.

He didn't need to call his parents to verify what she'd said. Amelia had always been true to her word, and she was a good person, free of bad intent. And that was why it hurt the most, he supposed. Because every word that she said had tapped into his worst fears.

And every word she had said was true.

Of course his aunt and uncle would have tried to help. Deep down, he'd known it, even heard snippets of conversations, arguments between his parents, pleas from his mother. And wasn't that why his mother had shut out Bonnie? It wasn't because she was jealous. It was because she was ashamed. Embarrassed. And not because they lost the business and the house, but because they'd turned their back on family.

On this town.

He hadn't seen much of Robbie and Jackson's parents since he'd been back in town, and now as he pushed himself off the swing he decided it was time for a formal visit. The drive to town was short—too short to allow for him to change his mind, not that he would have. He'd waited too damn long to come back to this town to leave with unanswered questions. Or any more regrets.

The carriage house behind the inn that was named for its very structure was where his aunt and uncle still lived, but despite taking a backseat to loyal staff at this phase of life, Matt knew that his aunt Bonnie would be in the inn, tending to the fire in the lobby or checking on guests.

Sure enough, he found her fluffing the throw pillows on the couch in the lobby, a warm and inviting space in rich wood tones and creamy, cottage-style furniture.

She looked up at him, surprised but pleased. "Matt!" She held her arms open wide, just as she had that first night he'd briefly seen her before going to the pub, after visiting Amelia in her kitchen. Was that only two weeks ago? It felt like a lifetime.

"Sorry that I've been so busy," he said, even though he knew that was only half-true. He had kept away from his aunt because it made him think of his mother, and it made him feel bad. But now he felt bad for other reasons, too. And he was sick and tired of feeling bad.

But Bonnie just smiled and motioned for him to sit. Like so many others in this town, she welcomed him as if he had just been here yesterday, not gone for half a lifetime.

Like Amelia had.

"You've been busy with this new resort development," Bonnie commented.

Matt nodded grimly. He had no doubts that his aunt knew every single detail. Word traveled fast, and Jackson was already aware of it before he'd had the chance to tell him directly. Needless to say, things were tense back on the home front. Might mean that was his cue to leave. To say goodbye to this town once and for all.

But everything he had done was to make sure that this time he could return and call it his own. Maybe, he thought, it had been there for him all along.

"Can I ask you a question, Bonnie?"

She nodded. "Anything."

"When my father lost the store..." He stopped, seeing the compassion in her eyes. "Did he and his brother...argue?"

Bonnie looked down at her hands and folded them in her lap. When she looked back up at him, he had the distinct impression that she had been waiting a long time to share her side of the story.

"Your father was a very proud man. He was the older brother, and he grew up thinking that he had to help take care of the family. For a while, everything was fine, and then the dynamic began to shift. We've been fortunate; our business here at the inn has always been steady, and we have waiting lists every weekend of summer, some weekdays too. And the local shops, well, they don't have that same sort of security." She smiled sadly. "Your father always loved old things. He loved finding them, restoring them, refinishing furniture that most people would throw out." She jutted her chin to the grand piano in the corner of the room. "He found that. Believe me, it didn't look like that when he did. But he made it what it is today and he gave it to us when we took over this inn. It's one of my most treasured possessions," she said quietly.

Matt admired the piano. He'd never known that his father had given that to his brother. "It's beautiful," he said.

Bonnie sighed. "We tried to help him. We offered up a loan, so he wouldn't think it was charity."

"And he didn't take it," Matt finished for her.

Bonnie looked at him sadly. "No. And by then, he was angry. He'd lost his house, and the store, and more than that, he'd lost something he loved very, very much."

"The antiques?" Matt asked.

"This town," Bonnie said. "Those old things he found and poured love into were a part of this town. And I think...I think he thought it failed him. That what he loved most about Blue Harbor hadn't been enough in the end."

Matt nodded. He understood all too well.

"He's a stubborn man," Matt said ruefully.

"Well, never give up hope," Bonnie sighed. "Life doesn't always go as planned. But sometimes, it leads us on the path we were meant to take."

Matt reached over and gave his aunt a hug. "Thank you, Bonnie. I've missed you, you know. I've missed all of you."

"We're right here. This is your home, too, Matt. You just have to remember that. There's still hope." Her last comment was more of a question, and she looked at him, as if she were searching his face for an answer.

One that he didn't have the answer to yet. He wanted to believe that everything would work out,

just as Bonnie said it would. And maybe, there was still a way that it could.

He left the inn and walked down Main Street, pausing at the road that led down to Amelia's café. He knew she'd be inside, tending to the last few tables or prepping for tomorrow.

He was so close, that he could be at the door in under a minute. See her, talk to her, try to get through to her. But he knew that now wasn't the time.

It was late. The sun would be up before he knew it, if he didn't beat it to it.

Best to get an early start if he intended to convince the mayor to put his plan into action.

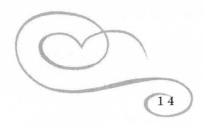

14

Amelia awoke to a pounding on her door. A hard, deliberate, urgent sound that wouldn't go away. Her heart sped up as she threw back the covers, realizing that it was still dark outside, and once glance at the clock on her bedside table confirmed that her alarm wasn't scheduled to go off for another eleven minutes.

She grabbed her once-soft terrycloth robe that Maddie had threatened to throw away once, flung it on, and pushed into the hallway toward the door.

Maddie was standing there, grinning wildly, already dressed for work. Her smile only slipped when she raked her eyes over Amelia's attire. "Still wearing that dingy thing? I thought I convinced you to get rid of it."

Amelia was hardly in the mood to justify her comfortable clothes, or point out that recent events just proved that she had no real point in making much effort. Really, Maddie should be happy that Amelia hadn't slipped on her ugly but oh so comfortable slippers. Yet.

"There isn't a fire?" Amelia was breathless. She waited for her heart rate to resume a normal speed as she fought off her annoyance at being interrupted. As it was, she had struggled to fall asleep, knowing that today was the day of the council meeting, when all her worst fears would materialize. Even a marathon of her favorite show couldn't calm her anxiety—or her dread.

And now she had been deprived eleven precious minutes of sleep, on a day she didn't even want to face, because Maddie couldn't wait to see what it brought?

"You won!" Maddie squealed, pushing past her into the house.

It took a moment for Amelia to register what Maddie even meant. But then it clicked. The contest. She'd actually done it.

*They'd* actually done it.

"That's...great news," she said, trying to picture how this would all play out. She'd have to find a new storefront soon. Her address would change. Should she be sure to tell the magazine that before they posted the information of her café for all to see? But she didn't even know where she would end up. None of the vacant storefronts looked appealing, and none were equipped with a full kitchen. This transition could take a while.

"You don't sound excited." Maddie looked disappointed, but Amelia couldn't bring herself to shake off the bad mood that had settled over her chest, weighing it down, landing with a heavy thud. This should be one of the happiest days she'd had in a long time. Just like that kiss should have been a happy day, too.

But how could she celebrate that her café was being recognized and honored when she might not even have a café much longer?

"I wish it was different," she said, tightening the belt around her waist. "A few months ago, this would have all felt exciting, like we were on the up and up. Now it feels like it's all just crashing down."

Maddie grabbed her by the arms, giving her a little shake. "This might be what you need to convince the town that you have a real, solid business that deserves your current location."

"And the empty space next door? And the other struggling boutiques behind Main Street?" She shook her head as she moved toward the kitchen in search of caffeine. "It's a lot of land."

Maddie closed the door behind her and followed her down the hall. "And I don't think many people would want to see some giant building erected in its place! Come on, Amelia. Don't let Matt take this from you too. You won the contest!"

"*We* won the contest," Amelia corrected, stopping at the kitchen counter. She managed a little smile, seeing how much this meant to her sister. She always knew that her family was her biggest cheerleader, but Maddie had been a special source of support over the years. Now, it was her turn to give back.

"I'm sharing the prize money with you," she said, and she held up a finger when Maddie started to protest. "Or I don't cash it at all."

Maddie gave her a rueful smile. "You drive a hard bargain."

"I learn from the best," Amelia replied, but her heart tugged when she recalled how exciting it had been to borrow that dress for a day. It had been a nice day.

"No," Maddie insisted. "I learned from the best."

Amelia busied herself making the coffee, using the good beans today, the ones that she usually saved for her days off. Normally this was mindless work, but today she struggled to concentrate on measuring the scoops, and the entire process felt labor intensive, and difficult. She looked at the clock on the wall, the one shaped like a strawberry that had been a Christmas gift from Maddie in younger years. She now had ten minutes to drink the cup that she usually had at the café. She didn't know how she would get through the breakfast service, much less the entire day. And a Friday, to boot, when they would be extra busy with all the summer tourists.

Once, that kind of work in the kitchen soothed her nerves and her worries, and grounded her.

Now, it no longer felt like her center. That café was her center. And that café was not going to be hers much longer.

"What are we going to do, Maddie?" she asked, her eyes filling with tears. She set her mug down on the counter, not even sure she cared if she started with her morning cup or not.

Maddie's smile dropped as they walked into the adjacent living room and dropped onto their favorite armchairs. On the mantle were framed family photos, most taken outside, all taken here in Blue Harbor. Amelia's eyes fell on the photo of her mother. It was one of her favorites of all time, taken in the backyard on a hot summer day. The girls were of various ages. Amelia was around nine. They were disheveled looking. Maddie was wearing a bathing suit that had been Cora's the year before. Britt was wearing cut-off shorts and a tank top. They were all barefoot, squinting in the sun. Their mother wore a big, floppy hat, but from under it, her smile was radiant. She had all her girls with her. All her little ones. That's what she'd called them.

Amelia wondered what had ever happened to that big, floppy hat. If it was tucked away, in the attic, along with the rest of their mother's clothes. The only thing they'd kept in place was their mother's apron, until Britt gave it to Maddie, where it belonged. Maddie kept their mother alive.

Just like Amelia had tried to do. For as long as she could.

"Sometimes I wonder what Mom would have said," Maddie said, staring at the same photo wistfully.

"Mom wouldn't have sat back and let someone take away something important to her," Amelia said. That much was for sure. She could still remember the time that Callie Lynch, one of the meaner girls in school, kept stealing the desserts from Amelia's lunch. The homemade ones that her mother lovingly tucked in their lunch bags every Friday, as a treat.

When Amelia had finally admitted to her mother what was happening, her mother ordered her to walk over to that girl and snatch it right back. Amelia had been startled. She'd just assumed she should tell her mother to stop making the effort for her. But her mother had insisted she would never stop making the effort for someone she cared about.

The next Friday, the girl had once again snatched Amelia's brownie. And that day, she was surprised to see Amelia stride over her to her table and take it right back.

She never stole another dessert. And Amelia learned a valuable lesson that day.

Her mother would always have her back. Even when she wasn't physically present to help her.

Amelia stood up, her decision made. "Do you think you can open the café today?"

Maddie looked startled, but nodded quickly. "Of course. Is everything okay?"

"No," Amelia said, as she moved toward the bedroom, her mind racing. "But it will be. It has to be."

She had only a few hours to convince Matt to change his mind about his resort. She didn't know how she would do it, exactly, but she had to try.

She owed her mother that much.

*

Jackson's house was on the edge of town, but Amelia took the car, getting her there in record time since the roads were still empty, most houses still dark through the windows.

It was probably too early to knock on someone's door, but she couldn't think about being polite just now. She hurried up the steps to Jackson's front porch and gave the door three hard taps. Then she waited. She checked her watch. By the time she'd changed, brushed her teeth and hair and—at Maddie's insistence—put on a smidge of makeup so she didn't look like she'd just rolled out of bed, time had passed quickly.

She was just about to knock again when she heard the turning of the lock. Her heart sped up as the door opened, to reveal Jackson standing barefoot in faded jeans and a white tee shirt. His hair was tousled, but he didn't look too annoyed to see her.

"I hope I didn't wake you," she said by way of apology.

He brushed a hand through the air. "I've been up for a bit. I was just making eggs, if you'd like some? Though they're probably not as good as the ones you make at the café."

She swallowed hard. "The café is actually why I'm here. Is...Matt here?" She searched the space behind him, but it appeared empty and quiet.

Jackson sighed heavily. "I heard about the plan for the resort. I'm sorry, Amelia. If it makes you feel any better, I made it clear to him how I felt about things."

It did make her feel better, even though she knew it hadn't made a difference. "Thanks, Jackson." Her eyes drifted into the living room behind him expectantly, hoping that Matt might appear.

"But if you're looking for Matt, he already left," Jackson said, frowning at her. "He was gone before I woke up. His car is gone, too."

She felt the panic rise up. The meeting wasn't supposed to start until nine—what could he be doing now, at this hour? It wasn't even seven!

"Did he say where he was going?" Not many places in Blue Harbor were open for breakfast, other than the inns, and those were usually just for patrons, and often, only offered on weekends.

Jackson's eyes filled with regret when he met her gaze, and he didn't need to speak for her to know what he was going to say. He rubbed a hand over his jaw, frowning.

"I'm sorry, Amelia, but I think he went to meet with the mayor. He mentioned something about it last night, but to be honest, I didn't really want to hear about it so I didn't ask him to elaborate. It's...a tough situation. A part of me is happy he's back, but the other part of me wishes the circumstances were different."

Amelia nodded, because she couldn't speak. He was with the mayor. They were cementing their plans before the town council meeting.

Her heart was pounding and her mind was spinning, and she could feel the hope slipping away. Still, if Matt was going to fight for what he wanted, then she was going to do the same.

"Thanks, Jackson," she managed.

He nodded. "Good luck, Amelia."

She managed not to snort. She'd need more than luck to turn this day around.

She got back into her car and drove off, feeling the gravel kick up as she took off down the driveway. Britt always teased her about her driving. Said she was too impatient. But today she was impatient. Time wasn't on her side. Not if she wanted to get to Matt before he got to the mayor.

The parking lot at Town Hall was empty, but she ran up the steps anyway, just to try the doors.

Locked. She dropped her hand, trying to think, but she was coming up blank. Defeat settled over her, and she willed herself not to cry, to tell herself that she'd done all she could. She'd run a good business. She'd won the contest! She'd done everything she could to keep that business steady. And now, it was time to let it go. At least, as it was.

Her sisters were right. As opposed as she was to change, she *had* changed, hadn't she? She'd been forced to, from a young age. She'd adapted. Kept moving forward. Even if it was with a broken heart.

She let out a breath, steadying herself, and turned to go back to the café. And that was when she saw him. Standing at the bottom of the stairs. A briefcase in his hand. A coffee cup in the other.

From the bagel place in Pine Falls.

So he had met the mayor, already. Off site. Out of town.

"Door's locked," she said, walking down the stairs slowly, eager to get away from him. He'd hurt her, in a way that she thought he never could, because even when he'd left town all those years ago, she'd known it wasn't his choice. But this?

This was his choice. More than that, it was his doing.

"Amelia," Matt said, as she brushed past him. "Wait."

"To say what? To hear what? To hear you say that you're sorry? That you don't want it to be this way?" Tears burned the backs of her eyes, but she refused to let them fall. This was no different than Callie and her special homemade treat, only this time, she couldn't just snatch back what was hers. Even if he could never understand the value. It wasn't just a café. It was...a part of her life. Just like he had once been.

And now he'd gone and taken that too.

"I don't want it to be this way," he pleaded, and something in his eyes, something in the agony of his expression made her stop walking, even though she knew that she should really keep moving.

Moving forward.

Because hope flickered, and despite all evidence to the contrary, she dared to think that maybe, maybe she could hold out for it. For a little while longer.

"Then don't do it, Matt. Don't try to push this through. It's one thing to build your resort, but to take down my café? And all the other businesses back there? It doesn't have to be this way!"

"It was never my idea to target that location," he said calmly. "You have to believe me."

She thought of the drawings, the way he described the project, the way his eyes came alive when he did. But she didn't need those facts to back up what she saw in his face. He was telling her the truth.

"Then why go along with it?" She stared at him, willing him to change his mind. "You know what that café means to me, Matt. And I'm not saying that your dream should matter less than mine, but...this is my town."

"It's my town, too," he said, his voice gruff. "At least, it was once. And I always wanted for it to be again."

She nodded slowly. And this was his way back, she supposed. As horrible and unfair as it was.

"It won't really be the town you loved so much once you make all those changes to it," she said, daring to look him hard in the eye.

He surprised her by saying, "That's right."

She blinked, unsure of what he meant by that statement. "And you're okay with that?"

"No," he said, as a little smile curved at his mouth. "I'm not."

Now Amelia's heart was pounding, but not with fear. She swallowed hard. Checked herself. She needed to think.

"I know you met with the mayor this morning, Matt. Jackson told me." She didn't mention the part about her going to the house, looking for him, hoping to change his mind or at least know that she had tried.

Matt set his bag down on the step and turned to her, huffing out a breath as he took a step in her direction. This time, there was nowhere for her to go. No stairs to flee. Just the wide-open lakefront at her back.

"I did meet with the mayor," he said.

And there it was. Suspicion confirmed. He'd had breakfast with the mayor. This entire conversation was pointless.

Only it didn't feel pointless. Not when he was looking at her like that. His eyes were soft, and a little sad. And his gaze was intent. She wanted to look away, and she did, only to find him still watching her.

"I pulled the project from the table," he said.

She stared at him, the shock no doubt obvious on her face. "Matt. I...You didn't." She blinked hard. He'd worked hard for that design. He'd been so excited about it. And now he was giving it all up.

And giving up Blue Harbor, too.

"No, Matt." She shook her head, setting her jaw. "You worked hard on that design. And it was a good idea. And that green space would be perfect for it!"

Matt shook his head. "The mayor is not willing to let anyone build on that land. He made that very clear. About as clear as he was about suggesting the land where your café is. It wasn't my idea, Amelia. You have to believe me. I never, ever would have initiated that."

Amelia shook her head. "Maybe I need to cut my losses. Like you said, it's the mayor who suggested the space. If it isn't you, it will be someone else. Build your resort, Matt."

"That resort doesn't belong there," Matt said, softly. "You do. And...I do, too."

She looked up at him sharply. "What do you mean?"

"I met with the mayor today, and I talked him into giving me a job as the town's zoning official. I can still use my architecture background, only this time I'd like to think I'm using it to protect all these wonderful, charming buildings that I loved so much growing up. Just like you reminded me."

Her breath caught in her throat as her eyes filled with tears. She fought off a smile, but it still managed to poke through. "I just showed you what you already knew, Matt."

"You reminded me who I was. Why I loved this town. Why I loved you," he said softly.

She blinked up at him. "Matt...But...your plans."

"Forget those plans. I was stubborn. Just like my dad. He might have lost his business and his home and his family, but I almost lost you. And I wasn't going to let that happen twice."

He reached down and took her hands, squeezing them tight.

"So you're staying?"

He nodded. "I finally made it back. Just not exactly the way I thought," he said, laughing softly. "I thought what I needed to make a success of this town was to change it. To undo what makes it so wonderful in the first place. But I realized that this town already has everything it needs. And I'm hoping...that so do I."

She sighed, wanting to open her heart just as much as she wasn't so sure she could dare to expose it again.

"I never meant to hurt you," he said softly. "I just...needed to find my way back. And you showed me the way."

She licked her lip, fighting off the tears, knowing that this was the moment she could open herself up to more than hope. To possibility.

And she knew that it was what her mother would want her to do. It was why, every Friday, starting the week that she had snatched her brownie back from Callie, her mother had added a second brownie to her lunch bag...to give to Callie.

Callie was now one of her friends. She didn't have a mother who baked. Her mother held down two jobs to make ends meet and was barely home to even cook dinner.

Amelia had been fortunate. Maybe even lucky. And when the bumps came along, she still had the joy of looking back on what she'd had once...and what she could still have again, she thought, looking up at Matt.

"This is where you were meant to be," she said. "Right here. Right now."

He leaned down and kissed her, and just like the other night, on the rock at the lake, it didn't feel like any time had passed at all. It felt as if she had found something that was hers all along.

When they broke apart, she looked up at him, needing to clear up one last thing. "But the resort..."

"Who knows? Maybe one day they will let that space open up for development." He grinned. "I'll be the first to know, won't I?"

"And the first in line?"

He considered this for a moment. "I have a different vision for that project now. Something that speaks from the past. Something that evokes the memories of everything that makes Blue Harbor so special."

"I like that," she said.

"I had a feeling you would," he said, leaning down to kiss her once more.

epilogue

It was a busy morning at the café, as it had been every day since the article had run featuring her café as the best in the state. Now it wasn't just the locals and tourists who came to try her seasonal fare, now she also saw repeat customers from neighboring towns, or people stopping over before taking the ferry to Evening Island.

And it was just going to get busier, Amelia knew, once Maddie left her to start her own bakery.

"I'm wondering if I should stay on to help a little longer." Maddie looked worried as she glanced through the window pass into the crowded dining room.

"Nonsense," Amelia said as she sliced a goat cheese and tomato quiche. "Matt made sure that you got the permit for the space next door and there is absolutely no reason for you to delay your plans any longer. Besides, I have already found your replacement."

"So soon?" Maddie looked just as surprised as she did disappointed, and Amelia had to turn her back to hide her smile.

"Sure did. Just to get me through the next month or so," Amelia said matter-of-factly, hoping that for once Maddie wouldn't be able to read the unspoken look in her eyes.

Maddie seemed to process this for a moment, as if it were suddenly clear that this was really happening, and that, to ensure it did, Amelia had all but ended her job here.

Maddie had needed a nudge, and now, Amelia was giving her a push.

She'd miss having her by her side each day, but having her next door was almost better. Maddie expressed the desire to just "look" at the empty storefront after the plans for the resort were dropped, and Amelia again insisted she have her half of the prize money from the contest, and Matt had jumped on the chance to approve a new business going into the space, and spent every spare second he wasn't holding down his new job, moving into his old house, and stopping by the café to visit, to draw up some blueprints for Maddie's new bakery. It all came together very quickly.

"You'll be so busy fixing that place up that you won't even miss me," Amelia said.

Maddie took a pan of her cinnamon rolls from the oven. Amelia knew she'd lose some business once those were sold next door instead of offered here at the café, but they'd already agreed to help each other, rather than compete. And considering that the blueprints Matt had drawn up included an internal opening that would allow patrons to come and go from the café to the bakery, Amelia knew she wouldn't have to worry about anything.

Well, maybe one thing.

"So, who did you manage to hire at the end of the season and on such short notice?" Maddie asked.

Before Amelia could reply, the kitchen door swung open, and Candy appeared, already wearing one of the blue and white striped aprons given to café staff.

"Yoohoo! I'm all ready for my first day!"

Maddie's eyes went large and Amelia just grinned back with a sigh. She set her hands on her hips and motioned to the station near the window. Candy's "famous" cheese biscuits were debuting on the menu today, and she'd made sure to stock all the ingredients ahead of time.

Maddie turned to her, her cheeks pink, as Candy filled the usually quiet space with her chatter. And all Amelia could do was shrug.

Things were going to be different from now on. But she'd come to realize that a little bit of change could be a very good thing, after all.

ABOUT THE AUTHOR

Olivia Miles is a *USA Today* bestselling author of feel-good women's fiction with a romantic twist. She has frequently been ranked as an Amazon Top 100 author, and her books have appeared on several bestseller lists, including Amazon charts, BookScan, and USA Today. Treasured by readers across the globe, Olivia's heartwarming stories have been translated into German, French, and Hungarian, with editions in Australia in the United Kingdom.

Olivia lives on the shore of Lake Michigan with her family.

Visit www.OliviaMilesBooks.com for more.

13442316R00146